Journey Tow

JOURNEY TOWARD RENEWAL

JOURNEY

TOWARD

RENEWAL

Meditations
on the Renewal of the Religious Life

by

Rev. Elio Gambari, S.M.M.

Translated by
the Daughters of St. Paul

ST. PAUL EDITIONS

NIHIL OBSTAT:
Rt. Rev. Matthew P. Stapleton
Diocesan Censor

IMPRIMATUR:
Richard Cardinal Cushing
Archbishop of Boston

September 13, 1968

Library of Congress Catalog Card Number: 68 - 24463

Printed by the DAUGHTERS OF ST. PAUL
50 St. Paul's Ave., Boston, Mass. 02130

FOREWORD

The Holy Spirit, source of inspiration and guidance for God's marvelous gift of the Second Vatican Council, should likewise be a source of inspiration and guidance for each one of us in our individual renewal: "Send forth your Spirit...and you shall renew the face of the earth." This earth which must be renewed, rejuvenated and transformed consists in ourselves, our institutes and the entire Church.

The Church emerged from the Council renewed according to the plan of God and His inspiration. We may look upon her as the new city, the holy city, the Jerusalem "coming down out of heaven from God," (Apoc. 21:2) renewed in order to renew the entire universe.

Nothing that the Holy Spirit has breathed into the conciliar documents must remain inactive. This gift of grace cannot remain sterile, but must be a germinating seed, productive in the Church and within each one of us. The Church, every institute, and each individual has the responsibility of bringing the Council into our lives, and of thus renewing ourselves. This is the will of the Holy Spirit; it is the desire, command and pressing need of the Church.

The Motu Proprio *Ecclesiae Sanctae,* issued by Pope Paul VI on August 6, 1966, has not only a juridical importance that obliges institutes to renew themselves, but also an importance for each one of us. This is stated in the opening words of the document's section on religious: "That the fruits of the Council may carefully mature...." So that the treasure of Vatican II may be received as a seed, protected and developed until it reaches maturity — and so that the Council may bear fruit in each one of us — the Holy Spirit must work within us.

The Council is a message of renewal, a message of holiness. "Unless this Council produces holiness," a Father declared in the council hall, "it will have done nothing; this time will have been wasted."

9

I believe that the spiritual exercises and meditations of men and women religious during this postconciliar era must be aimed at assimilating the true spirit of the Council, so that all the work for the application of conciliar norms carried out within their institutes may be prepared, animated and made fruitful by this same spirit. It is with this purpose that we seek to set forth the principles and criteria of the renewal and adaptation of the religious life.

We have endeavored to map out the "journey" that institutes and individual religious "under the inspiration of the Holy Spirit and the Guidance of the Church," (*Perfectae Caritatis*, n. 2) should make in order to attain to a more intimate communion with Jesus Christ in the Church and work together with Him to make Him present in the world in a special way.

This is the journey of the two disciples of Emmaus, which brought them to the recognition of Jesus, a consequent profession of faith in Him, and finally the proclamation of Him to others.

May we be guided on this journey by her who first chose to walk in the footsteps of Jesus, following Him in a life of virginity, of poverty, of obedience (cf. *Lumen Gentium*, n. 46).

— THE AUTHOR

CONTENTS

Chapter 1

RENEWAL IS PROGRESS IN THE RELIGIOUS VOCATION

The Council has been a new Pentecost, as Pope John XXIII was accustomed to call it, and as Pope Paul VI has repeated many times. We may further regard the Council as a movement for the rebirth of Jesus Christ in His Church, a movement to rediscover Him in ourselves and ourselves in Him, that we may be renewed in our faith and profession of love.

Pope Paul's pilgrimage to the Holy Land was a magnificent gesture; there, in Jerusalem and in Bethlehem, the Holy Father renewed the gift of the Church to Christ.

RENEWAL—AN ENCOUNTER WITH GOD THROUGH MARY

Our life in God in Christ Jesus is realized in a deeper knowledge of Him, in a living and more intimate love for Him, in a fuller participation in His mystery and in His life.

In this atmosphere of spiritual rebirth, the Mother of God is with us in a special way. Mary is still present; she is always present at the second coming of Jesus, that coming which takes place in our hearts. She was the first to be called upon to perform a mission intimately bound up with the designs of God—giving Jesus to the world. The renewal of the Church, of each institute and of each one of us will also be accomplished through her.

Encounter with Jesus Christ is the goal of renewal.

15

RENEWAL—TIME OF PRAYER

We must pray. In particular we should repeat the entreaties and supplications of the patriarchs, prophets, and people of God who awaited the promised Messia. For us the promise has been fulfilled. Let us pray that rebirth and renewal may truly be accomplished in ourselves, our institutes and the Church as a whole.

Spiritual exercises are times of prayer, and prayer is our weapon before God. *The Lord loves to let Himself be conquered by prayer.* Spiritual exercises in this post-conciliar era constitute a *powerful* period of prayer for ourselves and, above all, for the entire Church.

We are on retreat, and the Church is on retreat within each one of us.

Mary most holy presides over these spiritual exercises and helps us to understand what renewal of the religious life actually is. She gives us not merely a speculative knowledge of it, but rather a *practical and concrete* vision, which makes us penetrate more deeply into that great reality, and permits us to translate into action the renewal willed by the Holy Spirit for His Church, for our religious families, and for each one of us.

RENEWAL—ADHERENCE TO THE DIVINE WILL

Renewal is actualized and concretized in the enrichment of our own religious vocation, that is, in the fulfillment and complete development of our vocation, thus causing it to bear that fruit which the Lord, having called us into the institute, expects of us.

The religious vocation is a seed planted in a soul by God. It is not the product of human action or of environment; rather, it is a divine gift, a seed which must be sheltered, protected, and developed that it may bear fruit, and *all* the fruit that it should—the hundredfold.

Renewal is progress in our vocation, so that it may bear the fruit which the Lord, according to His designs, expects us to produce in His vineyard, the Church.

The Lord deals with us with great gentleness, with much respect and trust; He awaits our response. He does not run us like machines. He has given us intelligence, will and heart, and the potential of living a divine life.

With the religious vocation He has given us the possibility of living like Him.

Throughout article 46 and all of chapter 6 of the "Dogmatic Constitution on the Church," *Lumen Gentium,* there is a recurrence of the concept of religious life as the closest configuration with Christ, a configuration duplicating and reproducing the image of Jesus in the consecrated soul, assimilating it to Him living and operative in the entire Church, and establishing the most intimate of communions with Him.

Renewal means "measuring up" to Jesus, becoming similar to our blessed Lord, from whom flow those energies —those graces of light and strength—which enable us to conform ourselves ever more closely to Him who has called us to live in His house, so that we may keep in step with the designs of God. The Lord has a plan for each of us. He who knows each individual, knows each of us thoroughly; He is concerned about us, His chosen ones, far more than He is concerned about clothing the lilies of the fields and feeding the birds of the air. In His goodness, He has willed to associate us with Himself in the realization of His divine plan, in the unfolding of the history of salvation.

Renewal means full and constant adherence and correspondence to the designs of God, in such a way that what He wills for us and expects from us will daily be accomplished.

More than looking about in order to revise structures and forms and make them better suited to the life and demands of our times, *aggiornamento* involves looking to the design of God, a plan always new for us and, day by day, moment by moment, relevant to us.

RENEWAL—AGGIORNAMENTO OF THE RELIGIOUS LIFE IN ALL ITS FULLNESS

The concern of the Council was precisely this: *that we renew ourselves in order to keep up with the design of God,* so as to correspond fully to what the Holy Spirit wills from His Church, from religious institutes, and from each one of us.

What is the motivating force behind this renewal? It is this: the vocation is not a past event, a call which came to us at some point in our life's history, many or few years ago, and which we accepted; it is not an event of a day or moment, but a *continual and ever-present grace,* unfolding, unwinding; nor is it only one grace, but rather an abundance of them, a chain of graces originating in the bosom of the Most Holy Trinity, incorporating us into the plan of God, and being actualized in the Church, through our own institute, day by day, moment by moment.

We must be ever more deeply convinced of the here-and-now reality of our vocation. The mystery of Jesus, too, had its moments in time: the incarnation and paschal mystery which we recall and celebrate, but His mystery continues, since it must enter into all present-day realities, permeating them, and uniting them to itself.

Thus, renewal is the acceptance and welcoming of all the powers bound up with the vocational gift. The religious vocation is Jesus, coming to us, poor, obedient and chaste, in every moment of our day and of our existence; it is Jesus becoming incarnate and transfusing His life of poverty, chastity and obedience into us. In every moment we should live the mystery of the incarnation with full correspondence.

In a memorable congress of the sisters of the Archdiocese of Milan, on February 11, 1961, the then Cardinal Montini applied the words of the "Hail Mary" to religious women. "I greet you," he began, "I greet you, full of grace — you who have the Lord in your hearts and who among all women are blessed, since you are the disciples, daughters, devotees, enthusiasts and friends of Mary most holy."

The religious vocation is fullness of grace, full acceptance of grace in such a way that the consecrated soul has no gap, no emptiness, no space which is blank, much less black; there is no shadow, no hesitancy which sets limits to the fullness and continuity of the realization of God's design.

Renewal *is fullness; it is totality.* Indeed, totality is the chief characteristic of the religious life. Surely everyone should live totally for the Lord; nevertheless there is in the religious life a totality which singles it out and characterizes it: the gift to the Lord of an *undivided heart*, a heart handed over entirely to Him, without passing through any creature. This is the surest and quickest way to go to God, because it is total. The heart is undivided.

Renewal is fidelity to this wholeheartedness, to this enduring, intense totality, which prolongs itself and continues in every instant and in each of our actions.

On profession day we offered our all, in joy of heart; we gave ourselves into the hands of our superiors and through them into the hands of the Church which had placed us on the altar, and we offered our all, *without reserve*. It is because of this that profession is a holocaust. But such totality should be lasting and ever-present.

RENEWAL—SPIRITUAL YOUTH

Adaptation to the plan of God surely requires adaptation to the needs of the times, but this signifies complete and lasting accord with, and full adherence to the divine designs in the here and now. And this means *youthfulness*.

Renewal is the perpetuation of youth: "To Him who gives joy to my youth."

"He is the king of the ages," declares the Easter liturgy, and while pressing the grains of incense into the paschal candle in the form of a cross, the priest says: "Christ yesterday, Christ today, Christ always and throughout the ages."

"I am not the God of the past," the Lord says, "but the God of the present. I am not the God of the dead, but of the living."

"I am who am," Jesus repeated to St. Catherine.

Renewal may also be called rejuvenation, or perpetuation of youth. In the Lord we are always new. Our vocation is always a vocation in the present.

Why is the Blessed Virgin always young in pictures? Why does she look so youthful in Michelangelo's *Pieta?* Because virgins never grow old!

Freshness and youth stem from the living of one's vocation in the spirit of continual renewal, that is, as the vocation should be lived today, according to the plan of God, with dynamism and an intensified interior aspect. Jesus will not first be met on the streets amid hustle and bustle. Yes, we will encounter Him thus *also*, but not *firstly;* we will find Him within ourselves before all else. This is the requisite for meeting Him in our work, in others, in things — everywhere. The kingdom of God is within us.

RENEWAL—ENCOUNTER WITH JESUS

Before all else, renewal is *conversion to Jesus*, encounter with Jesus. Our gaze should be directed toward Him, our ears attentive to hear Him, our heart attuned to His and one with His.

Renewal is a *communion with Jesus* encountered within ourselves. It is a returning to Jesus in order to return to ourselves. This will enable us to meet Christ in the poor, in the suffering, in the sick, in the physician, in the patient's relatives, in the adolescent, in the infant, in pupils, in parents, and in those whom we see on the streets, in whom, unfortunately, we do not meet Christ because we pass by indifferent.... Never should a consecrated soul pass by a brother, indifferent.

We must meet Christ in others, after having met Him in ourselves and after having met ourselves in Him.

The religious life is characterized by directness, since we bind ourselves to a complete donation to Jesus, and therefore to others. From the Lord the religious comes down to people and things.

RENEWAL—INTERIOR DYNAMISM

Renewal is *dynamism*, that is, movement, activity, change, development and efforts carried on with fervor, desire, yearning. It is well to reread *Ecclesiam Suam,* "Paths of the Church," which is not to be viewed as separate from the Council, since it is one with it. In this encyclical, the Holy Father presents the Church in the above-mentioned attitude of yearning, of anxiety, and of generous and almost impatient need for renewal and amendment of the defects acknowledged in her interior examination before her mirror, which is the model Christ left of Himself. It is a sort of renovating force, obliging the Church to take another look at herself in order to transform herself; it is a dynamism of fervor leading to continual enrichment.

RENEWAL — PERSONALITY DEVELOPMENT

Renewal is the *development of our personality*. It is the perfection of maturity. It is continual, total, here-and-now fidelity.

Our personality expresses itself in our insertion into the plan of God, with love and totality. This requires becoming aware of what we are in God's plan, so as to attain perfection, in accord with the full stature of Christ.

If the religious life is the fullest, closest, most intimate conformity to Jesus, renewal will be nothing other than a revesting of ourselves with Christ, thus reproducing His image in a manner more living, full and real.

The postconciliar age is a fatiguing age, since it calls for a more intense effort, a more knowing and all-embracing commitment, but it is also a glorious era. We should be most grateful to the Lord for enabling us to live in it. Privileges, however, entail responsibilities.

Let us ask the Mother of God to empower us to understand and actualize this renewal of the religious life. Let us entrust ourselves to her unceasing maternal activity.

CHAPTER 2

RENEWAL IS FIDELITY TO EVERYTHING THAT CONSTITUTES THE VOCATION

Being committed to renewal, spiritual exercises are a means of rejuvenation. We should emerge from them young again in our spiritual and religious life.

This is an image corresponding to reality. The Church emerged from the Council rejuvenated. Let us recall St. John's vision in the Apocalypse: the new Jerusalem, the holy city coming down from heaven renewed, to make all things new—to rejuvenate all mankind.

We must incorporate ourselves into the Council and assure our life of a perpetual youthfulness. The religious life cannot grow old; otherwise it would no longer be life. Our consecration to the Lord must be intensified day by day.

We must know the striving for perfection which the Council asks us to renew, so that it may become a reality in our daily life, a desire, a yearning, a need, a reality not fleeting but permanent; an enthusiasm not of a few days only, but a passion, a love satisfied and realized in our life throughout the year.

The reality of the Council becomes our reality as well. The Holy Spirit will help us to have more light, which should convert itself into warmth and more fervor, which should transform itself into a life of commitment.

RENEWAL—ELIMINATION OF HABITUAL MEDIOCRITY

Spiritual exercises constitute a new beginning for the living of our religious life, especially in its contact with the

Lord. They intensify life, and especially in this postconciliar period they should set it aright by eliminating every encrustation which has formed upon our life of consecration. Although the religious life in itself does not grow old, in actual fact, in us it could.

Necessary, then, is a renewal which will bring us to eliminate anything inappropriate which may have attached itself to us.

Pope John XXIII declared that the Church of the Council feels the need of renewing herself, just as a ship often needs a new coat of paint in order to be renewed, while at other times, instead, it needs a good scraping down, simply because the placing of layers of paint one on top of the other has produced encrustations.

We should be honest with ourselves. Perhaps we have established ourselves in a certain manner of living and now go ahead in it habitually, without noticing that we have almost come to a standstill, or have diminished the flow of grace; we have our own *modus vivendi*, an habitual style, and we live completely by this and that is all, whereas in reality we belong to a state tending toward perfection.

We note that in the conciliar documents, mention is no longer made of the state of perfection. One of the reasons is that by talking about it so much, we run the risk of believing ourselves to be perfect although we are not, and of not setting to work with fresh vigor to tend towards perfection. Our whole life is a continual striving to revive the grace of the vocation in us, for the good of the institute and of the Church herself.

RENEWAL—A PERSONAL TASK

Renewal is a personal affair; it touches each one of us and calls for our active participation. The spiritual exercises require in us and from us a sincere, honest, objective scrutiny, in order to draw practical consequences which extend to the Church and the institute through each one of us.

The Church is the union of the children of God, and the institute is a body of chosen souls called to perfection — spiritual perfection. To think that renewal is for others would be a form of escape. Before it is for others, it is for us, each one of us.

The spiritual exercises call and recall thoughts of the overall view of our life, but summon each one to his active task, that the plan of God may be fulfilled in us.

Perhaps our customary attitude has been one of passivity, of letting ourselves be led. Meanwhile, one of the Council's innovations has been to summon everyone to the active role proper to the members of the Church, from the least to the greatest; it urges an attitude of active collaboration. The Council speaks of this in its passages on the formation of the clergy, and in the documents on the laity and the ministry and life of priests, where we find frequent repetition of the exhortation actively to participate, to do things, since all are called upon to perform their own tasks.

There are not two groups, one passive in outlook and the other active. All should be active, reflective, dynamic participants; that is, all should be attuned to the plan of God, which is continually unfolding.

It is upon *interiority* that we must insist, and it is precisely to interiority that we are repeatedly summoned by the Council.

Let us think of the Holy Father's address on obedience, which is an adherence accompanied by an internal conviction and a docility implying effort. Obedience is completely an interior undertaking. Today so much is said of personal activity in the world, yet perhaps there has never been so much passivity, spiritual inertia and conformity. It is necessary to be active, and the precise weapon for the combat is interiority.

RENEWAL—FIDELITY TO ONE'S OWN INSTITUTE

If the object of renewal is fidelity to one's vocation, the substance of renewal corresponds to that of the vocation itself: a call to likeness with Christ, to fidelity to the living of Christ as He presents Himself in the individual institute.

The special charism of the institute is none other than the spirit with which Christ is lived in that particular institute.

Every Directory delineates a special character or style which is to be penetrated, conserved, assimilated and translated into life.

We must insert ourselves into the Church — nowadays this integration is much talked about — but how should we do so? In accordance with the spirit of our institute.

Our *specific vocation* is a new status which integrates us into the Church, and *the more we belong to the Church, the more we will be ourselves,* according to the spirit of the founder, who was moved by the impulse of the Holy Spirit.

We owe fidelity to the rich spiritual heritage of our own institute.

Spiritual exercises also aim — and we shall say this right away — at renewing ourselves in our love for the Mother of God. The Council has not taken anything away from Mary Most Holy; rather it has lit another light in her crown, adding a new star to it by bringing to the forefront her maternal role with regard to the Church.

Thus called for is dynamic, complete fidelity to the entire content of our vocation, in all its dimensions and extensions. The vocation is wholly a chain of graces, since it comprises both a structure and a flexibility which animate the whole of our person and the whole of our life, shaping them anew.

RENEWAL — MATURATION OF BAPTISMAL GRACE

The conciliar documents *Lumen Gentium* (n. 44) and *Perfectae Caritatis* (n. 5), tend to show the bond which links the Christian and religious life. They emphasize their intimate connection. Since it is the full flowering of baptism, religious life enables baptismal grace to bring forth its best: maturation, the growth of Christ until His stature is attained.

The religious life takes over our whole Christian life to invest and revest it with a new dynamic vitality and to shape it anew.

This is the strength of the religious life. It brings the whole of the Christian life into its action.

We will better understand religious life by recalling, with the Council, the priestly, prophetic, kingly and eschatological dimensions of the Christian.

Chapter 4 of *Lumen Gentium* treats of the priestly, prophetic and kingly dimensions of the Christian people as participation in the life of Christ; chapter 6 of the same constitution further explains to us that the religious life in itself elevates these dimensions. Indeed, the religious takes every phase of the Christian life and makes it the sole reason for his being, for his life.

The religious life is *fidelity to the priestly dimension* of the Christian life, elevating it and making it a liturgy. Every Christian should be a liturgy of prayer and worship, but the religious makes his life one act of continual worship. The religious life is a liturgical state, an exercise of the priesthood of Christ.

The religious life is *fidelity to the prophetic dimension;* in fact, it is a *sign* recalling and revealing Christ to the world, since it is full participation in His life and His being.

The religious should be an *ostensorium,* as it were, in which the Church presents Jesus, praying, tending the sick, staying among the children, going about doing good to all, ever obeying the will of His Father.

Renewal in religious life also involves *fidelity to the apostolic dimension.* The Council has underlined the apostolic dimension of the entire Church, not to be understood as exterior action so much as communication of God through various activities.

Finally, religious life is full, *here-and-now fidelity to the eschatological dimension,* by virtue of which it proclaims another life and anticipates another mode of existence—the celestial. It is an anticipation of the future life in which no one will marry, own property or do his own will.

RENEWAL—ECCLESIAL LIFE

Binding considerations arise from these reflections: renewal is fidelity to the religious life in all its dimensions; it is fidelity to its bond with the Church, a vital tie which reflects the tie between Christ and the religious, between the Church and the religious.

Number 44 of *Lumen Gentium* contains a statement rich in light, warmth and responsibility: *we concretize and express the presence of Jesus in His Church.* Our life is the life of the Church. And chapter 8 of *Lumen Gentium* states that the Church has attained her perfection in and through Mary. In Mary the Church has produced her best; she has expressed herself in the most perfect manner. The Mother of God is both mother and daughter of the Church.

Thus our renewal is the renewal of the Church precisely under the aspect of the presence of Christ in the Church, and Christ is present in the Church in a special way through religious. The more we are religious, the more Christ will be present in His Church.

Christ wills that His presence and His action be made explicit in His Church by generous souls who have left all in order to follow Him, who have given themselves to Him with undivided hearts, and who therefore constitute a more efficacious and real presence of His apostolic action, the more each of them lives by Him and for Him.

We are not the only ones making the spiritual exercises, but the Church is making her own spiritual exercises in us, and in us she wishes to renew herself; Christ is making the exercises with us, for He wants a richness in us, a more complete expression of Himself. Therein is to be found a great source of light, warmth and life, which aims to flow out through our action and find its fullest expression through our more generous correspondence. From these spiritual exercises, we should emerge transfigured.

CHAPTER 3

THE DYNAMICS OF RENEWAL

We have indicated the substance of renewal, in relation to the substance of the religious vocation.

In order to actualize this renewal, it is helpful to ask ourselves just what task we must accomplish.

What does the Church expect of us?

What undertaking does it ask of us?

MEDITATING THE CONCILIAR DOCUMENTS

The implementing norms of the decree *Perfectae Caritatis* have been issued. Some norms were already contained in the decree itself. These two sources enable us to see that the first task to be taken in hand is a study and examination of the conciliar documents and of our own lives. In order to enter into the spirit and movement of the Council, we must know its mind and will.

Let us make the conciliar documents the object of our study, a study which should be meditation, prayer, docility to the Spirit of the Lord, and openness to all inspirations, so as to know both the will of God, explicitly set forth in the documents, and the spirit which animates the documents.

It is needful to know the letter of the documents and their various statements, since we should not reconstruct the Council according to our own viewpoints. Some individuals cite the Council not as it is, but as they see it, as if to justify their own positions or disseminate their own ideas.

All the documents should be studied well, but especially the two which concern consecrated life – the Constitution *Lumen Gentium* on the nature of the Church and the decree *Perfectae Caritatis* on the renewal and adaptation of the religious life—together with the implementing norms for the latter, *Ecclesiae Sanctae.*

Almost all of the conciliar documents refer to religious. The "Decree on the Pastoral Office of Bishops in the Church," for instance, presents religious as the bishop's collaborators rather than as his subjects, declaring that the bishop should have particular care for them. The "Constitution on the Sacred Liturgy" and the "Dogmatic Constitution on Divine Revelation" also speak of the religious life. Even where religious are not mentioned explicitly, they are still present and involved, since they are at the center of the Church, in the heart of the Church, and everything that concerns the Church is of particular interest to religious. All the documents, therefore, are to be studied and meditated.

ABSORBING THE SPIRIT OF THE DOCUMENTS

We must seize the meaning, content and substance of these treasures, and above all their spirit, that supernatural impulse which gives the documents life and transcends their letter.

These realities are the subject of experimentation more than of formulation; however, this does not mean that each one should interpret them in his own way. Nevertheless it is true that something should be grasped, understood and tasted, and this is the spirit which vivifies the documents and shines through them like a watermark held up to the light. The implementing norms, too, have spiritual implications; thus it is well to meditate on their meaning and spirit.

ATTUNING OURSELVES

We must measure our life, attitude, spirit and conduct as persons and as members of our institute, all in the light of the documents and at the mirror of the spirit emanating from them. First and foremost, this study, this task, this confrontation and examination are for each of us.

The third subsection of *Perfectae Caritatis*, n. 3, calls for a suitable revision of constitutions, directories, custom books and prayers in the light of the Council; but necessary first is an accurate examination of ourselves to see what there is within us which does not conform to the spirit of the Council.

The first question will be this: "What in our constitutions, in our institute and in myself is not in harmony with the letter and spirit of the conciliar documents?" It would be presumption to believe that there is nothing dissonant in us, as if we have already attained perfection, or have preceded the Council, or have already brought ourselves into complete conformity with the Council.

The purpose of examining the documents is to attune our mind, life, dispositions and spirituality to the conciliar wavelength.

The sphere of endeavor which opens up here cannot quickly be exhausted, rather it embraces our entire life. It is a work of vivification to bring into mind, will and actions all that the Holy Spirit has breathed into the conciliar documents.

It is not enough to say: "I have nothing within me that clashes with the Council." We must bring our life into step with the Council, and to do this we must pass beyond the letter of the documents and review our soul and our conduct.

These spiritual exercises should bring about a growth of our religious and apostolic spiritual life; they must make us assimilate the spirit of the Council, so that it will be the Council of our aggiornamento.

Such an examination should cause us to suppress not only whatever is contradictory to the Council, but also whatever is not corresponding fully: that certain egotistic opinion of our own holiness, which would wish to make the Lord all ours, our own monopoly excluding everyone else; that egoism, that preoccupation with self, that enclosure within self which harmonizes not at all with the spirit of that Council which opened to humanity a more expansive vision of the universal fatherhood of God.

Everything within us which does not completely conform to the spirit of the Council has to be removed, giving place to an ecumenical outlook, to participation in the liturgical movement, and to the study of Sacred Scripture. A work of revision, correction and completion should be going on within us so that the ideas, statements and initiatives which emerge from the conciliar documents may be integrated into our own personality.

The Council will become part and parcel of our life, if we keep our gaze fixed on what it is and on what we are.

WORKING IN DEPTH AND IN OPENNESS

What are the dynamics of the task of renewal — dynamics which we find in the Council and which should be reproduced in us?

Renewal and adaptation present themselves to us as constant activity in two directions: one vertical, or in depth (renewal), and the other horizontal or in openness (adaptation).

The first direction is clear from the documents, inasmuch as they place the Church in a condition of returning to her sources. For us there should be a continual return to the fonts of the Christian life and the origins of our institute.

Thus the decree *Perfectae Caritatis* speaks of returning to the true wellsprings of the religious life: the Gospel and our origins, the original spirit of our institute.

Such renewal and adaptation call for a constant and continual adhesion to the basis of our religious life, Christ Himself.

Many interpret renewal and adaptation only as an outward thrust, as an opening out to the world, forgetting that the Council calls for a constant, continual return to our blessed Lord before opening out towards the world.

One cannot go to the world if he has not first turned to Christ, if he does not have Christ to give to the world. When we will have established ourselves in Christ more completely, then we will be able, more surely and calmly, to launch out in the second direction — the horizontal — which brings the Church's presence into the world of today.

Into the world we should bring only Christ, in His evangelical message, re-expressing what Peter said and did before the temple gate called the Beautiful: "Silver and gold I have none; but what I have, that I give you. In the name of Jesus Christ...arise!" (Acts 3:6) Said Pope Paul to the United Nations, "I have come to bring you the ancient and ever new — Christ!"

The religious, too, is called to go into the world, but to bring Christ and to meet Him. This will not be possible unless one is rooted in Him, in His Person, unless he allows Christ to take possession of him. The world, then, will receive Christ if we have gone to Him first, and we will find Christ if we are grounded in Him.

Renewal is the vertical direction, the movement toward Christ; adaptation, on the other hand, signifies our orientation toward the society of our day.

In order to be genuine, this second movement must also be characterized by the Spirit of Christ. In the environmental, social, and cultural circumstances to which we must adapt ourselves and our institute, we must see the signs of God — that is, the plan of God — in the world. But this point must be clear, that the Council is not calling us to make the contemporary world's customs our own. Even though adapted to the present day, our encounter with the world does not imply conformity with the world. Our adaptation does not mean acceptance of the world's thoughts and desires. What is to be gathered from the milieu is the good, the beautiful and the appropriate, insofar as it expresses the will of God. In a word, we must discover the signs of God's plan and respond to those demands which express the will of God.

Our vocation is not something abstract; it is active in the world, in the surroundings of today. Our religious life is unfolding at a determined time and for the present day and the present environment; here we must be able to discern the finger and will of God and adapt ourselves to existing realities, insofar as they reveal to us the plan of God, that design which we must make our own.

The Church must enter into the society of today; she must become incarnate in the world of today, and not to the detriment of her wealth but in order to give of her wealth.

Religious institutes must adapt their own customs to the circumstances of today, in the sense that they must become involved in whatever is beautiful and divine, to express and carry out the design of God.

Such aggiornamento is not a compromise between the demands of our vocation and the demands of the world. It is not a compromise in which something is yielded up from prayer life or mortification, from obedience or renunciation, in order to obtain something else. No. Aggiornamento in its various phases does not mean the diminishing of the exigencies of a vocation. The vocation should find its full gratification even amid the surroundings of today—responding, however, to those necessities which are in the plan of God today.

Never should adaptation be taken to mean *restriction* of the obligations of the vocation; never should our vocation of witness be marred. The religious in the world cannot be like everyone else, not because he wants to appear different but in order to be really himself. The religious in the world has the *function of a sign,* of a motive force, and thus he must be in the world without being of the world.

MAKING ALL CONVERGE TO CHRIST

What is to be corrected in regard to aggiornamento?

Certainly, account must be taken of physical, psychological, moral, cultural, environmental and other necessities, but up to what point? We are living the crucial point of the application, where true necessities may be confused with pretexts. Real needs, in fact, are sometimes hidden under compromises, pretexts, justifications of weakness, mediocrity and fear of exertion.

Renewal and adaptation must be expressed in a constant vertical motion. Let us first go to Jesus, and from Jesus to the world, returning from the world again to Him. Only if our encounter with the world has Christ as the point of departure, and only if the encounter with the world spurs us to return to the Lord—only then will we be on the right way, and only thus will adaptation be authentic.

But if there were halfheartedness in the Christ encounter, in our approach to the Lord, then aggiornamento would not be completely sincere.

To acknowledge new methods and resources, to alter certain practices, is to change form, not substance. With regard to the substance, nothing can or should be changed.

Renewal should produce adaptation as its fruit; thus flower and fruit are both expressions of the same rich interiority.

In this as well, Mary is the perfect model.

After the incarnation of the Word, she who loved recollection so much, emerged from her home and journeyed to her cousin Elizabeth to bring Jesus. She is the living image of our aggiornamento. We, too, can be called to new forms of apostolate, but they should show forth a better way of bearing Christ; only thus do new forms have reason for existing. Let Mary, then, be our model, both in renewal and in adaptation.

CHAPTER 4

GUARANTEES OF THE AUTHENTICITY OF RENEWAL

The Second Vatican Council's deepest concern was the renewal and adaptation of the Church. Both of these are greatly emphasized with regard to us religious.

We pause to study the meaning of such renewal and adaptation, and their dynamics, as set forth in the conciliar documents. These are to be studied, meditated and penetrated so as to derive from them the directives and spirit for a fruitful renewal and a true aggiornamento of the religious life.

RENEWAL SHOULD FIND CONTINUITY IN ADAPTATION

As we have said, there is a vitality in the work of renewal, a double force, a double movement — one motion, in a sense, vertical or in depth, and the other horizontal or open; from these two movements arise the two components of the renewal and adaptation of the religious life.

We are not speaking of parallel lines, but of two lines, one of which continues the other and results from the other.

With regard to the first component — renewal — we, both as persons and as an institute, must respond to the obligations manifested in the life of Jesus, in His response to the religious vocation given Him by His Father.

But such a vocation should concretize itself in a determined environment, in a given moment in time; thus, the religious life needs to confront those obligations which really express the times in which we are called to live our own religious life.

Our apostolate, for example, should be the continuation of that of Jesus. Now this apostolate must be carried out in the midst of the men of today, according to their ideologies, psychology, education, tastes, necessities, methods and means. Thus, the apostolate is to be accomplished with the means most suitable and fitting for contemporary civilization. There are particular modern exigencies in technology and formation which cannot be overlooked, much less disregarded.

The obligations arising from close attachment to Jesus are substantially the same, but should be fulfilled in different ways. They will be subjects of renewal. The obligations stemming from apostolic action, on the other hand, will constitute subjects of adaptation.

There cannot be discontinuity, much less lack of harmony, between renewal and adaptation — between response to the demands of Jesus, the Religious of the Father, and response to the demands of the religious life in the modern world.

INTERIORITY SHOULD HAVE PREEMINENCE IN RENEWAL

It is not unusual that religious find themselves at a fork in the road — a crucial point — and ask themselves: "How and how far should I respond to the obligations of the surroundings in which I find myself? For example, regarding mortification and self-denial: in an era when self-assertion is made much of, and the meaning of the cross is so little heeded, must I rule out penance, mortification and renunciation?"

On the practical level, in regard to relations with our families, we now have received some suggestions even from the Church herself. Some institutes have modified their regulations in this regard. Should we see in this a return to primitive fervor, or must we give a new meaning to relations with our families?

Adaptation does not reflect fervor unless it is a continuation of interior renewal.

But it is difficult to distinguish clearly whether a change is due to fervor or to a certain relaxation. It is so easy to cover up, excuse or justify alienation from what the spirit of mortification suggests to us, by pleading the need for openness, aggiornamento and adaptation. But there can also be an enslavement to a pleasant custom to which one is attached, or to a tradition which is meaningless for today but which one does not care to give up.

We may find ourselves hesitant or uncertain. Hence, the necessity of a serious and deep interior renewal.

To resolve this problem, it is well to emphasize the words of the first paragraph of *Perfectae Caritatis,* n. 2: this renewal is to be accomplished *"under the inspiration of the Holy Spirit and the guidance of the Church."* This is of utmost importance.

In regard to the religious life in general and every religious institute in particular, the Council has emphasized that such a life is the fruit of the Holy Spirit. *Lumen Gentium,* n. 43, declares that the Church "under the inspiration of the Holy Spirit" interprets, regulates and guides the religious life; n. 44 states that the religious life "clearly shows all men both the unsurpassed breadth of the strength of Christ the King and the infinite power of the Holy Spirit marvelously working in the Church." And again it is "under the impulse of the Holy Spirit" that religious rules are given approval.

Also, *Perfectae Caritatis,* n. 1, declares that religious institutes have been founded "under the inspiration of the Holy Spirit," and all those who are called and who consecrate themselves to the Lord in a special way, "driven by love with which the Holy Spirit floods their hearts," live more and more for Christ and for His Church.

Religious institutes are not merely the product of a temporal necessity; they also have their basis in a charism of the Holy Spirit just as the Holy Spirit is at the root of every religious vocation, which is an inspiration given by Him in some mysterious way. The religious life is a charismatic life; thus, it is grounded in the action of the Holy Spirit, in a special gift, in an invitation and singular impulse of grace. This charismatic character does not, however, detach one from the authority of the Church, nor render him independent of those to whom the Holy Spirit has given guiding positions in the Church. This specific action of the Holy

Spirit requires from us a great readiness to welcome the impulses He will give us during our spiritual exercises. Such docility to the Holy Spirit ought always to go hand in hand with our religious life.

The religious life is animated by a supernatural motivation, since its principal source of inspiration and regulation is not our own taste, preference or pleasure, but the taste of God, the preference of God and the pleasure of God, of which the Holy Spirit is the expression.

At the foundation of the religious life then, should be a supernatural motivation. The motivation of the life, sentiments, actions and conduct of a religious should be found not in self, but in the inspirations of the Holy Spirit who should consequently direct the renewal of the religious life.

What place have we given the Holy Spirit until now? What docility have we shown to His appeals and impulses?

Too often the religious life is accused of *legalism,* and perhaps there is a little truth in this accusation, since we may have looked more to the letter than to the spirit.

RENEWAL SHOULD BE GUIDED BY AUTHORITY

What is to be said of the attitude of certain religious who believe themselves moved by the Holy Spirit outside of the authority and will of the Church? Under the pretext of docility to the Holy Spirit, they seek to withdraw themselves from the authority of the Church and detach themselves from their superiors who are the Church's lawful representatives. We must reemphasize that only under the guidance of the Church is one certain of being in the truth. This is so since, as *Perfectae Caritatis* states, the influence of the Holy Spirit is not separate from the "guidance of the Church."

As the documents declare, the Church was entrusted by her divine Founder to the authority whom He erected ever to be "the pillar and mainstay of the truth" (cf. *Lumen Gentium,* n. 8).

Promised and sent by Jesus, the Holy Spirit has given the Church pastors to guide it as His authentic representatives. The Holy Spirit works in such a way that His authenticity can be ascertained through lawful superiors.

Some individuals in our day speak of religious life as if it all had been changed, as if obedience had to be re dimensionalized and fidelity to observance were no longer necessary. Thus, stealthily is being introduced an attitude similar to that of some Protestants who believe themselves to be in direct communication with the Holy Spirit, and say that they have no need of mediators, that is, of authority.

Allow me to repeat it. The Church is the instrument of the Holy Spirit, and when the Church speaks, the Spirit speaks. Therefore true updating and adaptation are those inspired by the Holy Spirit and directed by the Church.

The formula with which the Holy Father promulgated the conciliar documents always included those two elements, the Holy Spirit and authority: "And we, with the apostolic power conferred upon us by Christ, together with the venerable Fathers in the Holy Spirit...."

The Holy Spirit assists the pastors of the flock of Christ directly, and the Spirit cannot contradict Himself. Never does He speak against authority, and authority acting lawfully will never be in opposition to the Spirit; the two factors merge together, and the Holy Spirit and authority harmonize, blend and complete themselves in the activity of enlightening and guiding.

On our part, this calls for a policy of listening to the Holy Spirit and an attitude of docility expressed in the supernatural motivation basic to the entire task of aggiornamento. The Holy Spirit will always be with us, as He is with the Church.

The dispositions for adaptation should be acquired by all, but the factor without which adaptation will not be made is authority. The extent of adaptation must be determined by authority. Each one may and must set forth his suggestions, but it is not up to each individual to make a classification as to what is important in the institute and rules, and what is so unimportant that it may be kept or done away with at will. No, the norms of adaptation are to be determined only by competent authority.

It is well to insist on this point, because the danger is more than hypothetical that there will be individuals in a community who will act as judges, who will set themselves up to evaluate the laws currently in force in the institute, ready to lay them aside or change them of their own accord.

Let us recall that when the Holy Spirit works *He makes us docile and obedient.* When we will be called in to express our opinions on one point or another, we will do so, but with humility and docility to the Holy Spirit who is present in the lawful authority. Then we will accept whatever the competent authority will establish.

With such a spirit of union in searching and in docility, there will be no danger of divisions. Rather, this auspicious renewal and adaptation will bring about a closer union of souls and greater fervor in the community.

There are so many crises in this postconciliar time, but what will be the means for foreseeing and resolving them? *Docility to the Holy Spirit and obedience to the Church.*

The "Decree on Priestly Training" declares that obedience places us in communion with the three divine Persons and causes us to share in the life of God. Obedience is the gift of our will to God, represented by authority. It may be said that disobedience is like an excommunication which cuts us off from life.

Renewal and adaptation should be a work of obedience and of submission, which, without excluding active and personal participation, renders the religious docile to the action of the Holy Spirit and to the guidance of authority. This authority always emanates from the Holy Spirit through those whom He has placed in charge of religious families.

What gratitude we owe to God for having given us authority and especially for having given us the Pope, the *guardian* of the truth. The Holy Father asks us to pray, for not all is bright on the horizon, and his paternal and pastoral soul is suffering and grief-stricken.

CHAPTER 5

THE GOSPEL—
PRIME SOURCE OF RENEWAL

The renewal of our life should be fostered by the Holy
Spirit. We ask the most holy Virgin to obtain for us the
grace of enlightenment, that we may understand what
God wants of us.

Renewal must be animated and nourished by the Holy
Spirit, just as our institute and our vocation have sprung
forth from Him. The Mother of God will obtain the *grace of
counsel* for us, so that we will understand what is needful
for our renewal and clearly discern what truly corresponds
to God's plan and our rejuvenation.

Mary, the Spouse of the Holy Spirit, will also obtain for
us the *gift of fortitude,* so that, once we have understood
what God wishes from us and what we should do, we may
be docile, prompt and diligent in acting. Above all, we
need the gift of fortitude understood as docility, availability, readiness, generosity and constancy in persever-
ance.

Many graces have been received in the annual retreats
of years gone by, and many good resolutions made. Something was done indeed, but is it not likely that the Lord
expected more?

And during or after our retreats in this post-conciliar
era, which we have termed special, what does He expect
of us? If the Lord causes thoughts of our responsibilities and duties to stir within us, He helps us at the same
time, since His assistance is a grace of enlightenment and of
energy transforming itself into ardor. The Holy Spirit will
surely pour out His gifts upon us, provided we count on

41

Him, not on our own abilities and resources; above all, He will be especially active insofar as our institutes are dedicated to the Blessed Virgin in a special way and a characteristic and intense Marian devotion has been instilled in us.

The Spirit blows where He finds His beloved spouse, the Virgin Mary; certainly, therefore, He will work intensely. Wrote St. Louis de Montfort: "When Mary is rooted in a soul, there are produced such marvels of grace as only she is capable of producing, for she alone is the fruitful virgin whom no one ever has resembled or will resemble in purity and fecundity" (*True Devotion*, n. 35).

Having seen how aggiornamento should be carried out under the influence of the Holy Spirit and the guidance of the Church, we now look at the sources, the principles which should nourish, regulate and strengthen the renewal and adaptation of our own personal life and that of our institute. They are set forth in n. 2 of *Perfectae Caritatis*.

CONFORMITY WITH CHRIST

Before all else we must remember that renewal consists in a continual return to the sources of every form of Christian life and to the true spirit of religious institutes. Constant devoted attachment to the wellsprings and roots of the religious life should regulate and direct every authentic renewal.

The principles set forth in *Perfectae Caritatis*, n. 2a, are a guide to a genuine renewal, and consequently are to be held up as the norm of our undertaking.

"Since the ultimate norm of the religious life is the *following of Christ* set forth in the Gospels, let this be held by all institutes as the *highest rule*."

This basic principle brings us to the sources of our religious life: configuration with Christ, conformity of life with Christ.

From this it follows that the principle of renewal is a clinging to Him, a communion with Him; it clearly follows that the religious life will correspond to its purpose and express all its riches if those who are called to integrate themselves into this mystery remain in a close communion of thoughts, sentiments, will and life with Him who is the Religious of the Father. Our religious life is an incorporation into Christ. We are like the branch; if the sap rises and is transmitted from the trunk to the branch, we live of the trunk. We are like the branch which must transform the divine richness flowing from the trunk and express a particular aspect of that vital fluid: the aspect of poverty, chastity and obedience; that is, of exclusive and total love of the Lord.

THE FOLLOWING OF CHRIST

Fidelity to this way of life, inspiring every act of existence, is obtained through union with Jesus Christ, who manifests and gives Himself so powerfully and effectively in many ways, the most efficient and eloquent of these being the Gospel. The source of our renewal is Jesus, as He presents Himself to us in the Gospel.

It was not by accident that every general meeting of the Council Fathers began with the enthronement of the Gospel following the celebration of Holy Mass. This ceremony indicated that the entire source of the conciliar endeavors was to be Jesus, and Jesus as presented in the Gospel. This principle holds true for the entire Church, but especially for us, since the religious life is, in essence, an evangelical life. Very often we notice in the lives of the saints that it was the reading of the Gospel which made them aware of God's call and attuned them to receive the word of vocation transmitted by the Gospel.

The ultimate norm for renewal is the *following of Christ*, as presented to us in the Gospel. When this was developed in the conciliar commission, one of the Fathers pointed out that there is no divergence between the Gospel and Jesus, because the Gospel *is* Jesus—Jesus who has spoken, who has acted. But the Gospel does not tell us everything about Him; much has been gathered up and set down, but not all, and what is stated in the Gospel is little when compared with the majestic, divine Person of our Lord Jesus Christ. It is only in this that there is a difference between the Gospel and Christ. Christ is the Good News; He is the message; He is the life; "I am the way, the truth and the life" (Jn. 14:6).

To return to Christ means to go back to the Gospel, and to go back to the Gospel means to return to Him. "Many things yet I have to say to you," said Jesus to His own, just before His death, "but you cannot bear them now. But when he, the Spirit of truth, has come, he will teach you all the truth.... He will receive of what is mine and declare it to you" (Jn. 16:12-15). We will better understand Jesus in the light of the Gospel, which will be explained to us by the Holy Spirit with the help and guidance of that infallible authority which is the Church.

EVANGELICAL LIFE

The Council has led the Church, and especially us religious, back to the Gospel; our constitutions should therefore express the principles of the Gospel, and formation should include the study and penetration of the Gospel from the novitiate on. The first paragraph of *Ecclesiae Sanctae,* n. 16, states:

"Study and meditation on the Gospels and the whole of Sacred Scripture should be more earnestly fostered by all members from the beginning of their novitiate."

And the second paragraph of *Perfectae Caritatis,* n. 6, expressly declares that religious "should have recourse daily to the Holy Scriptures, in order that, by reading and meditating on Holy Writ, they may learn 'the surpassing worth of knowing Jesus Christ.'"

Similar expressions are to be found in the "Dogmatic Constitution on Divine Revelation," which is one of the most important conciliar documents, since it makes clear the necessity of close attachment to the Lord, as He manifests Himself to us in the Gospel He entrusted to the Church.

The Gospel is the Church's heritage, and has been entrusted to her that she may guard and protect it, make it known and help it to be lived. The following directive frequently recurs in the conciliar documents: the faithful, priests and religious must nourish themselves at the table of the Word of God and the Eucharistic banquet. God is truly present at both tables; therefore, our well-being consists in nourishing ourselves at these inexhaustible fonts of the divine Word and the Eucharist.

Perfectae Caritatis, n. 6, and the "Decree on Priestly Training" emphasize this concept.

It is essential frequently and fully to have recourse to the Gospel; there is a great deal of searching for books — prayerbooks and new meditation books — but the book *par excellence*, the book of life, always remains the Gospel. Up to now, perhaps, we have not plumbed its depths thoroughly, and have not derived from it all the enlightenment, strength and nourishment that we need.

The religious life is the complete Gospel, both in what it commands and in what it advises. We religious take the entire Gospel, down to the letter.

Chapter 5 of *Lumen Gentium* states that everyone, according to his own circumstances, must live by the spirit of the evangelical counsels; however, the religious takes upon himself the entire Gospel — in its doctrine, commands and counsels — all, both letter and spirit. The religious is called to become more like Jesus, and to become a living Gospel, as it were. The consecrated life is the evangelical life.

May the Holy Spirit and the most holy Virgin help us to understand the Gospel and to nourish our meditation from this perennial font. Jesus, speaking to the Samaritan woman beside the well of Sichem, also teaches us: "He who drinks of the water that I will give him shall never thirst" (Jn. 4:13), because here is the perennial font of life. And if we say with the Samaritan woman: "Lord, give me this water," Jesus will say to us: "Take up my Gospel."

CHAPTER 6

THE GOSPEL—ULTIMATE NORM
OF OUR CONDUCT

We have meditated on the basic source upon which our renewal should draw: the Gospel, principle of all Christian life, font of the religious life, and in a special way the guiding norm of us religious. We must never set the Gospel aside. The Gospel is the ultimate norm of our conduct. The Gospel should vivify our religious life, as well as all of religious formation and the constitutions.

New, at least in part, is the statement of *Ecclesiae Sanctae*, n. 12, that the constitutions should contain *"the evangelical and theological principles of the religious life and of its union with the Church."* The Gospel is to be the font of our thoughts, judgments and actions; it is to be our standard for the appraisal and evaluation of everything.

We recall the example given us by the Mother of God: she knew Sacred Scripture thoroughly, especially the Gospel—not the fourfold gospel, but *the Gospel Itself—Jesus*. How meaningful for us is the attitude of her who conserved in her heart everything that she heard, saw and learned from Jesus, and pondered upon it.

She was in intimate contact with Him who is the living Gospel, the Word of God; she was a faithful echo of Jesus, but not an echo repeating only the final syllables; insofar as a creature is capable of reflecting the Creator, all of Jesus was reflected in her.

When the woman of the people exclaimed, upon seeing the Messia: "Blessed is the womb that bore you, and the breasts that nursed you," and Jesus replied, "Rather blessed are they who hear the Word of God and keep it" (Lk. 11:27-28), He made known His Mother's fidelity in listening to the Word of God and assimilating it into her own life. This is what impresses us the most about Mary; this is the most compelling summons to draw near to the Gospel and to bring it into our lives.

LIVING GOSPELS

We religious should write the Gospel in our life and conduct; in other words, we should become living Gospels.

Just as we often see the mysteries of faith portrayed in the stained glass of cathedrals, and the Gospel illustrated in the mosaics of basilicas, inviting the faithful to read the Scriptures, learn from them and love them, so—and to a much greater degree—should we be living witnesses of the Gospel to our brothers.

Through the lives of religious the Church should be able to show Jesus more clearly every day to Christians and non-Christians alike: *Lumen Gentium,* n. 46. It is the will of Jesus: "You shall be witnesses for me...even to the very ends of the earth" (Acts 1:8).

The Gospel should be the source, the unit of measurement, the standard of our renewal. We should truly welcome the Council's exhortation to nourish ourselves on the Gospel, for it is from the Gospel that we can learn how to attain *the most excellent knowledge of Jesus.*

We should welcome the biblical or scriptural movement into our lives for one purpose especially—learning in order to teach others that Jesus is way, truth and life.

In the conciliar documents the Church refers to the Gospel frequently. It is her wish that we also, docile to her directives, always return to this wellspring, so that it may motivate our conduct, as the law of our life.

The three numbers of *Perfectae Caritatis* regarding the religious vows are introduced by a reference to the Gospel. In order to show us the Founder of religious life and its origin, *Lumen Gentium* cites the words and actions of Jesus as handed down to us in the Gospel.

It has been said by some that the religious life does not have its foundation in the Gospel. In the past there was a movement among some Protestants to do away with the religious life almost as if it were not biblical; history tells us how the Council of Trent worked in this field. Even in our midst now, there are similar mistaken notions—unfounded opinions which do not acknowledge the evangelical origin of the religious life. Yet we have it in the Council documents, especially in *Lumen Gentium,* chapter 6, n. 43.

WITNESSES OF THE GOSPEL

The Gospel gives us not only the words of Jesus, but also His actions. We have explicit evangelical words on chastity and poverty. While it is true that the Gospel does not contain any clear expression on full and absolute obedience as a counsel, we have the example of Jesus, the Word Incarnate, who was obedient to the extreme of holocaust. Thus the Council has led the religious life back to its evangelical nature—to its sources, which are: *the life, conduct and words of Jesus.*

The Council asks that the constitutions contain references to the Gospel, but first of all the Gospel should be brought into our lives and *lived in actuality,* in the language of deeds.

We have much to learn and to assimilate from the Gospel. Because this font is inexhaustible, we will not be able to accomplish everything in a whole lifetime. We must draw ever more deeply from this wellspring; we must be *the witnesses* of the Gospel.

Our every deed should be motivated by the Gospel—that is, justified and evaluated in its light—and whatever actions do not accord with the Gospel should be eliminated. The scriptural basis of the religious life was given more attention by Vatican II than by any other council. The measuring stick of our life should thus be the Gospel. Let us recall Simeon's words to the Virgin: "This child is destined for the fall and for the rise of many in Israel, and for a sign that shall be contradicted" (Lk. 2:34); that is, men will be known in God's sight as they are in reality. Those who become similar to Him will logically be with Him in the joyous resurrection and will be separated from those who are against Him, or, in other words, against the Gospel. "A sign that shall be contradicted," for He is to show how one ought to live.

DISCIPLES OF THE MASTER

We should therefore ask ourselves: What is there in my life which contradicts the Gospel? St. Louis M. de Montfort based his life on this standard: fidelity to the entire Gospel.

Our renewal must be a return to the Gospel: *we must be disciples and witnesses of the Gospel* in imitation of the Blessed Virgin, who was the most faithful disciple and witness of her Jesus, of the Word of God. She transmitted the word to the evangelist St. Luke.

In this matter of return to the Gospel, we have much to learn so that the Good News will truly be our nourishment and principle of life.

Nowadays, with the continual progress being made in biblical studies, uncertainty and something akin to fear wells up within us: what interpretation will be exact, what exegesis true?

We must not be too fearful. We need not approach the Gospel with the attitude of a scholar in history or exegesis, in order to assure ourselves of the authenticity of every passage, *but as disciples of the Master,* as disciples who are eager to know what the Master says. We must meet the Gospel *with simplicity of soul,* as the Church presents it to us, as she explains it to us. Yes, the Church desires that the Gospel be studied; that is, that effort be made to penetrate it more deeply, but the Church in no way doubts the Gospel.

We should be grateful to the Lord for His message, but also grateful to Him for having given us, in the Church, a wise, knowing and sure teacher.

DEVOTION TO THE WORD

The Church guides us in understanding her message, making herself the disciple of Jesus and making us more fully His disciples, too, through the liturgy, which has now given new emphasis to *devotion to the word*. This insistence upon returning to the Gospel does not imply that the Church has lacked esteem for the Gospel before, or had forgotten it; rather, this insistence was due to the forgetfulness of her children and to their neglect for this font of Sacred Scripture.

The Church has always had devotion to the word; in her earliest years she introduced its reading into the liturgy. Through knowledge of the word transmitted to us, and through Jesus present in the Gospel, the Church readies us for our encounter with Jesus present in the Eucharist. In all this we must allow ourselves to be helped by the Mother of God.

We should think and act like Mary, and reproduce her life in ours. She kept the Gospel living in her heart, meditating upon it, practicing it and translating it into her life. More than anyone else, then, she can bring us to know and savor the Gospel; she can guide our hand to inscribe the Gospel on our life. This should be one of our resolutions: to remain Mary's disciple in order to read, understand, savor and live the Gospel.

CHAPTER 7

THE ORIGINAL INSPIRATION
OF THE INSTITUTE

We cont.nue to meditate on the sources of our renewal. We have considered the Gospel, prime wellspring of the entire religious life. The second source to which the Council refers is our religious family. Already in the first line of *Perfectae Caritatis*, n. 2, it is stated that the renewal of the religious life involves a continual return to the sources of every form of Christian life, and to the original inspiration of the institute—that is, to the original inspiration regarding the birth of the institute itself; to the impulse given the founders by the Holy Spirit; to the sharing in the divine plan by those who were called to erect the institute.

ORIGINAL INSPIRATION

The expression *"primigenia"* leads us back to the moment in which the founder received the call and inspiration from God to enrich the Church with a new religious family. Thus at the source of the religious life is to be found the heart of God, the breath of the Holy Spirit.

The term *"primitive spirit,"* on the other hand, means the atmosphere, fervor and generosity which were present in the religious family in its first years; it refers to the period in which the institute's original inspiration was translated into action.

Every founder has foreseen and wished his creature to be as it appeared in the mind, heart and design of God; he has sought to apprehend the image of this creature, his religious family. It is important to retrace our steps to that initial moment in which the plan of God was actualized.

Original inspiration surely implies the communication of the plan of God to the founders; however, this inspiration must above all be obtained from the mind of the Church, which has approved the religious family. The origin of the institute is to be found in the mind of God, communicated to the founders and ratified by the Church.

In speaking of the founders, perhaps we think only of that man or woman chosen by God to bring a certain institute into existence; and perhaps we do not give enough thought to the Church, who is, formally, the foundress of that religious family, inasmuch as she has given life in raising up the institute and approving its constitutions. The original inspiration to which we are asked to return brings us first to the mind and heart of God, then to the mind and heart of the Church, and to what the founder expressed as having been manifested to him as an inspiration from on high.

Each founder underwent many anxieties and trials. He had deeply at heart the Church's approbation of his family, sprung up like a mustard seed cast upon the good ground of the Church and growing up with such simplicity and humility in circumstances sometimes commonplace and normal, accompanied neither by astonishing events nor by revelations.

PERMANENT REALITY

The simplicity, modesty and obscurity accompanying the rise of an institute form part of the original inspiration in the mind of God and in the minds of His human instruments. The Lord has so many ways of making Himself known. It is necessary to know, take up and assimilate this inspiration, so as to relive it, for it has not ceased to be; it communicates itself to us also.

Just as the grace of the vocation was not merely a fleeting moment which ended when we responded to it, but is instead a chain of graces, so also the original inspiration is not something of the past, but an enduring reality which is the soul or spirit of our communities — as it were, the breath which gives our communities life.

Even if this inspiration does not reach our ears, there is, nonetheless, a presence of the voice, thought and heart of our founders which lingers on in our houses, which accompanies us in life, especially in our novitiates, juniorates and generalates and in those members who hold positions of responsibility. We must listen to this voice, for we must be instruments who promptly, generously and docilely put the original inspiration into effect, as the founder did. It is needful to have the original inspiration clear, especially today when each institute is called upon to look at itself and its structures anew.

MANY-FACETED HOLINESS

In explaining the return to the original inspiration, *Perfectae Caritatis*, n. 2b, states:

"Let their founders' spirit and the special aims they set before them as well as their sound traditions — all of which make up the patrimony of each institute — be faithfully held in honor."

The passage begins thus:

"It redounds to the good of the Church that institutes have their own particular characteristics and work."

These words are to be insisted upon and emphasized. During the preconciliar period, according to scattered voices, it seemed that there was a tendency toward the standardization of all institutes. A certain fear crept about, a desire to recombine the energies which had been dispersed throughout authentic communities — of nurses, for example, or of teachers — in order to build up a veritable army of religious.

The clergy, too, sometimes forgot that religious institutes are not merely the product of an age, sprung up as a way of satisfying the necessities of an historical moment or the needs of a specific environment. Rather, religious institutes have their motive in the Church and their source in the mind and heart of God; they have arisen for the good of the Church. Every institute has its *raison d'être*, which is the holiness of the Church, the apostolate of the Church, the beauty of the Church.

This concept is set forth in *Lumen Gentium*, which states that the variety among the Church's religious families is the work of the Holy Spirit. *Perfectae Caritatis*, n. 1, observes that this diversity of religious families has the purpose of adorning the Church, that she may appear in her beauty as a bride adorned for her husband, and that the manifold wisdom of God may shine forth through her.

Pope Pius XII spoke of the Church as a garden filled with a variety of flowers; in these flowers he saw the many religious families.

In an audience, Pope Paul VI declared that the variety of institutes, manifested also by the habit, calls to mind the image of the Church, rich in many beautiful virtues and in countless ranks of saints, represented by the various religious families.

This manifold variety is also meant to enrich the Church with the necessary means for doing good. The Church is the mother of the saints, and must make the heavenly city incarnate in the earthly city; to do this she needs many means, resources and workers. Now the religious institutes provide the Church with means, resources and workers specialized for every sphere of apostolic ministry.

The variety of religious institutes, then, stems from the Church's need to reveal her own spiritual riches and the manifold wisdom of God.

DYNAMIC FIDELITY

So that the Church will be faithful to her vocation and mission, she asks us to be faithful to our vocation and to the mission of our institute; these are the vocation and mission of the Church herself.

Love for one's own institute resolves itself into love for the Church. It has been said that it is necessary to eliminate corporate egoism. In reality, the restriction of horizons to one's own institute is now less clear cut. The Council helps us to see the institute within the framework of the Church. The religious institute is part of the Church; therefore, it is not to remain closed within itself, but is to be itself in the Church.

When in a recent discourse Pope Paul VI asked the Jesuits: "Do you wish to remain yourselves?" he was asking the same thing of all religious: to remain faithful to their original spirit, to the spirit of their beginnings and of their founder—in other words, to that attitude of mind and heart which characterized the origins of the institute and which is the external expression of its inspiration.

Perfectae Caritatis, n. 2b, refers to the heritage of one's own institute—that is, to the spirit, the objectives, and the sound traditions which make up its special character, characteristics and nature.

We are at a crossroads. On the one hand, the Church asks us to be faithful to ourselves, and on the other, she summons us to carry out opportune adaptations and to adjust ourselves to new circumstances, to review constitutions, directories, prayerbooks, and customs in order to adapt them to the present day and age. We are at a crossroads between excessive immobility and a mobility just as extreme.

The Church asks for fidelity to ourselves and to our institutes—but a fidelity which is dynamic and vital, and which distinguishes essential or primary values from the secondary and accessory. She asks, therefore, a fidelity which calls upon us to conserve what is fundamental and substantial, and also, through fidelity to ourselves, to eliminate whatever in our way of thinking, praying, living and working is accidental, short-lived or even harmful.

SAFEGUARDING THE SPIRITUAL HERITAGE

In the conciliar documents there is a constant exhortation to *safeguard the institute's special character*, and also a pressing recommendation to *adapt the institute to new circumstances and conditions of life*.

How is this adaptation to be achieved? Through fidelity to one's own special character, and always and only under the action of the Holy Spirit and the guidance of the

Church, who knows how to sort out the substantial from the accidental. The Church knows what is to be conserved and what is to be changed or replaced—in such a way, however, that the external expression always corresponds to the primitive spirit, to the founders' aims and to sound traditions.

By elements in the heritage of the institute are meant the original inspiration, the initial purposes, the goals to be attained and the sound traditions: whatever makes up the special character, characteristics and nature of the institute itself.

Every institute has its own nature and a distinctive primitive spirit: *of simplicity, of humility, of obscurity, of availability, of gentleness, of docility,* and so on. These are characteristic notes which must remain.

Elements in the special character of the institute are the aims and goals to be attained, understood as obligations—as duties which should be carried out by the institute itself and which should wholly occupy the members—such duties as: assistance to the sick and aged, education of children and youth, social help to orphans, parish activities, and so forth. These, too, must remain.

When it comes to the sound traditions, some difficulties may be encountered with regard to adaptation. Very clear ideas are needed here. Constitutions and directories are somewhat lean; the riches of an institute are not all contained therein. There is something which transmits itself from one generation to another; there is an atmosphere of fervor which draws near to the Lord and animates relations between religious and laity, between superiors and religious, among religious themselves and between them and superiors; there is a family spirit which binds the members of a community and is not formulated in the constitutions. This, too, is a sound tradition—the patrimony of the institute.

There is also a particular manner of giving oneself to others, of helping the sick and needy—a manner proper to the institute and difficult to express in writing and to state in formulas.

These sound traditions must remain. We must not be iconoclasts. There are values which have permanent force and must remain.

PRUDENT ADAPTATION OF THE ACCESSORY

And what, then, should be modified?

We are asked to adapt or redimensionalize certain customs, certain ways of doing, praying and governing which were good and effective in the past but perhaps are no longer so today.

The norms implementing *Perfectae Caritatis (Ecclesiae Sanotae),* state that those prescriptions which are no longer up to date should be suitably examined and suppressed. Something is no longer up to date when it has lost its power, when it is no longer understood, when it has an effect opposite to what was intended, or when it can be an obstacle to good. This may be clearly seen in *Ecclesiae Sanctae,* n. 17, which states that the religious life must always be *faithful* to its innate mission of witnessing.

The religious life is supernatural and it must maintain this characteristic. Assuredly, a hedonistic milieu no longer understands penance, mortification and renunciation. But does this perhaps mean that, just because this world no longer understands such factors, we must eliminate them from the Christian and religious life? It does not. This is not the spirit of the Council.

In concrete situations it is necessary to distinguish the signs of God's will in the times from signs of the world's wisdom or weakness. In distinguishing the essential from the accessory, let us always have recourse to the Gospel, with the assistance of the Holy Spirit and the guidance of the Church. We must never let ourselves be deflected from the spirit of the Gospel.

For example, the method of assisting at Holy Mass has changed. Therefore, some revisions are called for. If in the manner of giving directives, customs have been introduced which are no longer suited to the proper needs of the times, these, too, should be revised.

Superiors should be concerned about setting forth the will of God in a gracious way, thus reproducing in the government of the community the Blessed Virgin's way of acting. Authoritarian attitudes are not according to God; they have to be changed.

Different attitudes are not according to God; they have to be changed.

Dynamic fidelity is in order; this is vital to the true spirit of an institute. The tree which wishes to bear new fruit, lets flowers, fruits and leaves fall at the proper season, so as to be able to yield a new harvest.

The original inspiration, goals and sound traditions of an institute have such an inner wealth that they can be expressed in ways more suited to our times.

Such externals are what have to be adapted and updated, and these external expressions will be understood and grasped by those who have placed themselves in a supernatural atmosphere, fully ready—docile to the Holy Spirit and to the directives of the Church.

It would be disastrous if something of substantial worth were to be eliminated. For example, *silence* should be understood, viewed and practiced as a type of enclosure which allows one to draw near to the Lord and listen to Him; a little dissipation is enough to make one almost deaf to His voice. Thus, *discipline certainly should not be dropped.* Nowadays we hear: "Oh, the little things—why get lost over trifles? There's so much to do!" Let us proceed slowly. There may be some externals to revise; there will be others to adapt to some extent. However, we must not permit ourselves to be guided by the pretext of being more independent, or by the excuse of expressing our own personality.

Sometimes one hears: "Our religious are adults; let them make their own decisions." No, our discipline must remain intact, though some of its externals will change. Let the trellis be altered suitably, but without cutting away what maintains our contact with God. Great care is necessary, for we are treating with values which must be conserved.

Our fidelity should be dynamic; therefore it will be necessary to revise ways of acting, of managing and of organizing the community itself, in order to attain greater efficiency and to keep the sound traditions of the institute, since these latter are a precious part of the character and patrimony of the religious family.

CHAPTER 8

PARTICIPATION IN THE LIFE
OF THE CHURCH

We continue to meditate on what the Council has told us, so that we may incorporate into our lives the light the Lord has shed upon us. We encounter Him in the patrimony of the Council, and we hear Him now in the third criterion for the updating of the religious life – an aggiornamento which must flow steadily from the wellsprings of religious life.

We first examined the supreme norm of religious adaptation, the Gospel, and then the second, which is the original inspiration – the special treasure of each institute, the special way of living the Gospel which God has shown to us.

This original inspiration represents in the concrete the profile and lines to be stressed in imitating Christ. This profile and these outlines were manifested through the charism given by God to the founders, ratified and given to us through the Church, and present within our institutes.

PARTICIPATION IN THE CHURCH,
SACRAMENT OF CHRIST

The third principle of renewal is set forth in *Perfectae Caritatis*, n. 2c, which states:

"All institutes should *share in the life of the Church*, adapting as their own and implementing in accordance with their own characteristics the

Church's undertakings and aims in matters biblical, liturgical, dogmatic, pastoral, ecumenical,
missionary and social."

What we should above all derive from this principle is
the norm and duty of participating in the life of the Church
and of sharing in the life of our blessed Lord.

Vatican II concentrated wholly on the Church, and
therefore the task of adaptation and renewal must be centered on the Church, focal point of the entire spirit of the
Council's efforts. The spirit of the Council *emanates from
the Church and leads to the Church.*

As presented to us in the Constitution *Lumen Gentium,*
the Church has been shown as the point of departure
and the destination of all conciliar labors. It was the focal
point of the other conciliar initiatives, decrees and commissions.

The Council has chosen to respond to the question the
Church has asked itself: "What are you, O Church of
Christ?"

In the Council, the Church has willed to encounter
herself, in order to deepen her self-knowledge — in order
to acquire a more profound and intimate awareness of what
she is. The Church has acquired this awareness by viewing
herself in Christ and viewing Christ in herself. And Vatican II, the Council of the Church, mirrors the mystery of
Christ inasmuch as the Church is the Church of Christ.
The mystery of the Church is glimpsed in the mystery
of Christ. *"Lumen Gentium"* — these words present the
Church as a reflection of the light of Christ, a light shining
on the Church's brow. The most holy Council has intended
to illuminate the entire world with this light. The entire
"Constitution on the Church" aims at manifesting the profound mystery of the intimate relationship linking Christ to
the Church and the Church to Christ. It is said that the
Church is the extension of Christ, and, as it were, a second
incarnation of the Word.

In the mystery of the Church, Jesus, the Incarnate
Word, unites humanity to Himself in the union of a *mystical
but real person.* The Church is the Mystical Body of Christ;

in Christ, she is the sacrament of union with the Father, Son and Holy Spirit, yet also the sacrament of unity among all the children of God. The Church is the meeting ground of God and humanity, of humanity and God, and of all men who, as sons of God and of the Church, feel themselves brothers in Him. The Church is the mystery of Christ. In the mystery of the Church Jesus manifests Himself living and acting. The "Decree on Priestly Training" states that, in and by means of the Church, Christ continues His service to the heavenly Father Christ works in the Church and by means of the Church in the person of His ministers.

IN THE CHURCH, LIFE OF CHRIST

The Church is the means through which we unite ourselves to Christ and can live of His life, participating and sharing in His mystery. In the Church we are born in Christ and grow in Him; Christ is intimately united to the Church, and the Church is intimately united to Christ—and we are born and grow in the Church, receiving His own life.

Truly the mystery of the Church, upon which the Council has focused, is our light and our strength. It causes us to live a new life.

If the Church is the sacrament of union with God and with one's brethren, if it is the means through which we are born in Christ and live in Him, it is understandable that only in and through the Church is the religious to become configured with Christ and acquire a truer resemblance to His reality.

Thus, the Council has insistently stressed a reality which, although always believed and lived in the Church, needed to be better understood and more completely assimilated and lived. The Council wants us to encounter ourselves and Jesus in the Church, and witness to Him through an ecclesial life.

The Council has given the religious life a wholly ecclesial orientation. This is not a new perspective; it has always been felt. It is chiefly to be found in the prayer of the Mass of holy founders, where religious life's membership in the Church is focused upon: "O Lord," the prayer begins, "You enriched Your Church with a new religious family...."

Founders have always been aware of a particular bond joining them to the Church; they have always desired that their religious families be approved by the Church, and that they receive new life from her who is the one formal foundress of institutes.

Lumen Gentium, n. 44, declares that the religious state involves a special bond with Christ and a particular tie with the Church. A close bond with the Church is essential to a close bond with Christ.

The Christian life is also linked with the Church, but the religious life is accompanied by a new bond, which joins it to Christ and His Church, and makes the religious life perfectly Christian. The religious is bound to Christ and the Church in a particular and vital way. There are not two bonds, but only one, for the Church is Christ living and acting, who has united believers to Himself. They live of His life as a fruit of the redemption.

Loyalty to Christ is loyalty to the Church; love of Christ is love of the Church. These are mysteries which we must penetrate with the understanding of love, for they are mysteries in which we are implicated as part of the total mystery. Assuredly, we cannot exhaust the mystery; however, we must penetrate it, in order to be permeated by it and in order to assimilate it into our religious life.

WITH THE CHURCH, SPOUSE OF CHRIST

What is the purpose of this special bond with the Church? It is to make Christ more present in the Church, and the Church much more present to Christ.

Lumen Gentium, n. 44, contains such marvelous expressions as: *the more fully we will be religious, the more fully will we render Christ present to the Church and the Church to Christ.*

In the rite of the consecration of virgins, it is stated that, while matrimony brings to mind the bonds which link Christ and His spouse, the Church, religious profession, instead, concretizes and reinvigorates these bonds and makes them present here and now. This is a mystery about which we must think, for the Church's fidelity to Christ depends upon our fidelity. The Church's total gift to Christ is re-lived in our gift.

Through religious the Church succeeds in expressing her union with Christ. Through his or her profession, the religious concretizes the holiness of the Church. The Church is holy in the person of her members. To be sure, sanctity is hers because of her Head first of all, but she must correspond to this holiness through the holiness of her children, and she does so.

Lumen Gentium, chapter 8, declares that the Church has shown herself without a wrinkle, beautiful, pure and holy in the person of the Mother of God; Mary is she who has expressed the Church's holiness more fully than any other creature.

This is our mission—our task. The religious life, too, is a sacrament, a sign of the union of Christ with the Church and of the Church with Christ.

All this should arouse a particular enthusiasm in us, and should arouse a movement of fervor in the Church—through our renewal and sanctification, both of these understood as participation in the life of the Church and as communion of life with the Church herself.

THROUGH THE CHURCH, THE FRUIT OF CHRIST

The Church is the fruit of Christ. Born from His bleeding side, she should also, in a sense, be born from us. We should contribute to her holiness, which requires acceptance, commitment and fidelity in her members.

Popes Pius XII, John XXIII and Paul VI have told us that, although the Church's sanctity is assured by the holiness of her Head, a correspondence on the part of her members is also called for. The Church cannot be without wrinkle when her members do not act holily.

The Council states that the Church is composed of a divine element and a human element. It is precisely this encountering of ourselves in the Church and of the Church in us, which brings us to understand that we are not insignificant. This ecclesial perspective makes us aware of what we are in the Church; it obliges us to understand that the vocation and mission to which we are called is strongly binding, and that the future of souls is linked up with it.

Let us think of the Blessed Virgin's role in the plan of God. The religious vocation, too, has value not only for ourselves but for all of humanity.

Let us ask the Mother of God, who is Mother and Daughter of the Church, to help us better understand the Church.

The Holy Father compares religious souls with the Blessed Virgin, precisely in these two prerogatives of hers. According to their possibilities, religious also are called upon to live this double mystery of mother and child of the Church.

CHAPTER 9

THE AWAKENING OF OUR ECCLESIAL CONSCIOUSNESS

Let us meditate on our participation in the life of the Church. The head of the Church is Jesus, from whom everything flows; He has given all of Himself to the Church, having been immolated for it; with the Father He has sent it the Holy Spirit, the spirit of light and strength, the soul of the Church.

May the Holy Spirit aid us in grasping this mystery of grace and love. May the Virgin Mary, Mother of the Church, come to our assistance.

How beautiful it is to contemplate Mary in the Cenacle, in the midst of the apostles, the comforter of the Church which had just been born from the sacred side of Jesus. Mary draws the effusion of the Holy Spirit down upon the Church. She sacrificed her only Son for it; she who gave Him at the foot of the cross received the Church into her care.

It is certain that the Blessed Virgin will help us to understand our concrete participation in the life of the Church *in a practical way,* causing us to experience the Church as a point of encounter between God and ourselves, between ourselves and God, between ourselves and all our brethren.

THE CHURCH INCARNATE IN RELIGIOUS

The mystery of the Church which the Council has illustrated, under the inspiration of the Holy Spirit, is concrete and real; it has an immediate bearing upon us because we are part of it. The mystery of the Church causes us to encounter Jesus. There is in the Church a golden cord which binds us to the most holy Trinity and makes us share in the intimate life of the three divine Persons.

The Church is like a tabernacle in which we can live in the intimacy of the three divine Persons. Interior life consists exactly in this—a life of familiarity and intimacy with the divine Persons. The Church is the gateway to this life.

In the Church, moreover, we feel ourselves more closely bound one to another, with a tie stronger than that of blood, since the bond is the blood of Christ and the life of God. In the Church we meet all our brethren. The Church is the sign of the unity of all humanity. In her we meet redeemed brothers already enjoying life in Christ. We meet all those whom the Father is calling and who have yet to be redeemed even though the portals of salvation are already open to them. These brethren of ours must come into the home where their Father awaits them, in order to know, love and serve the true God as He wills to be adored and served.

If only we would reflect more that in the Church we meet our brethren so that they, too, can come to the knowledge, adoration and service of God.

In the Church we find light, strength and the true meaning of all our life. The Church embraces our entire existence, our every activity and expression of personality. She incarnates herself in our life, and desires to incarnate herself in society—in all the life of today—to transfigure it.

The Church opens herself and extends her hands to the world, in a gesture of expectation and invitation, in an act of embracing all humanity, just as Jesus on the cross stretched out His arms in order to embrace all.

Does it not seem that in the colonnade of Bernini in St. Peter's Square we can see this universal embrace of the Church and of Christ?

The Church is not of the earth, but she lives and hopes on the earth. It is here that she must carry on her mission, and she wills to transfigure our earthly life to make it a preparation for the life of heaven. There is a pilgrim Church, a suffering Church and a heavenly Church, but there is no separation between the pilgrim Church and the heavenly Church. The pilgrim Church is on the march toward eternal life and joy—in other words, toward the life of eternal companionship with the three divine Persons. If only we were to grasp this truth and penetrate this unique mystery more deeply, how filled we would all be with this eternal reality!

With good reason can Paul VI be called the Pope of the Church, both because of his first encyclical, "Paths of His Church," and because he has made the Church the focal point of his magisterium.

THE CHURCH

OFFERING HERSELF WITH RELIGIOUS

In the Church we find the *raison d'être* of our life, and especially of our life as religious. *Ecclesial awareness* should unify our life, in our relations with God, ourselves and our neighbor. The Church is the marvelous theme that gives unity, cohesion and consistency to our life. The Church is none other than the design of God unfolding and fulfilling itself here on earth; in it God desires to encounter humanity and humanity longs to encounter God.

The Church is an inner, mystic, supernatural reality, but it is also an external, visible, tangible and juridical reality. The Church has its divine element and its human element, its spiritual element and its tangible element, and we must incorporate ourselves into the whole of the Church's life, with the whole of our life, whether in the depths of our being or in the external expression of life: effort, activity, fatigue and labor.

Everything is to be integrated into the Church and lived as part of the Church.

At our religious profession we gave our entire selves with all our faculties and gifts of nature and grace; we pronounced the vows as bonds of our entire existence, and entrusted ourselves to the Church through our superiors.

The Church received our vows, profession and life and made them her own. From that moment on, our integration into the Church, which began with baptism, was strengthened and extended. Our life has been taken up by the Church in a way altogether special, and has been made her property. The significance of a public vow is this: in virtue of the profession received by a representative of the

Church, the vow is not only that of a specific individual, but a vow of the Church.

Lumen Gentium, n. 45, expresses this concept when stating that the Church accepts the vows and unites this offering to that of Jesus. In the person taking the vows, the Church offers herself to Jesus.

All this is not pure poetry. Although rich in poetry, this is a reality. In a certain sense, at profession we cease to be ourselves and become the Church. Our personality is not diminished by this fusion with the Church, but our "I" is stamped with the "I" of the Church.

It is said in the program of clerical formation that the young men must be imbued with the mystery of the Church. The priest becomes a person of the Church; he is the Church. The same can be said of the religious. In this ecclesial perspective, profession is both a destination and a starting point; we make ourselves the Church, fusing our life with that of the Church and fusing the Church's life with ours. We must be imbued with the Church. We must know, love and cherish our ties with the Church.

The ecclesial mystery shared in by us should also be the principle which gives unity, coherence and cohesion to religious formation and religious life.

The norms in *Ecclesiae Sanctae* for the implementation of *Perfectae Caritatis,* place great stress on the bond between the Church and the religious life. In order to be lived, this bond has to be felt.

Ecclesial awareness gives our religious life its true meaning. This awareness widens the horizons of a life which certainly is one of silence, modesty, obscurity and humility, yet at the same time incorporated into that of Christ—*a life hidden with Christ in God.* Ecclesial awareness opens the soul of the religious to the whole world, occupying and preoccupying us with the life of all humanity.

THE CHURCH COMMUNICATING

HERSELF THROUGH RELIGIOUS

Integration into the Church is a golden cord linking us with the life of God. It makes us sharers in the life of all men, sensitive to all the joys and sorrows of mankind, to the necessities of the suffering, to the problems of families, to the needs of the small and the great. Insofar as we are integrated into the Church and her mystery, to that extent we are open to the needs of the whole world. In the Church our vows and brotherly solidarity acquire meaning. Why does the world call religious "sisters" and "brothers"? It does so because the vows generate a new relationship in the bosom of the Church which makes us brothers. That is how our vows take on meaning in the life of the Church.

The vow of chastity, a bond with the Church and with all of humanity through the Church, appears in its positive aspect. Our house and family are the entire Church, not a limited group. All humanity is loved in the heart of Christ Himself, to whom we have given our heart.

The vow of poverty places us above struggles and controversies, to view the problems of mankind with the impartiality of the Church.

The vow of obedience becomes a means through which the life of the Church communicates itself to us while we place ourselves at the Church's disposal, so as to be sent out to others.

Instead of separating us from others, integration into the Church thrusts us out into the world. As the Church is not a separation, but is a congregation, an assembly, a community and a bond, so our profession, exactly because it integrates us into the Church, binds us to all.

In *Perfectae Caritatis*, n. 2c, we read:

"All institutes should share in the life of the Church, adapting as their own and implementing in accordance with their own characteristics the Church's undertakings and aims in matters biblical, liturgical, dogmatic, pastoral, ecumenical, missionary and social."

What horizons open themselves to our life, to our gaze, to our heart, to our activity!

Of the Holy Virgin—who consecrated herself to the Lord in poverty, chastity and obedience; integrated herself into the great mystery of salvation; and became Mother of the Church—let us ask the grace to understand something of this radiant mystery. Let us ask the grace of integrating ourselves into the masterpiece of the Church and making our life truly ecclesial.

CHAPTER 10

FOR ME TO LIVE IS THE CHURCH

The Council should incite us to reawaken our ecclesial consciousness, our ecclesial personality.

Our stress on Vatican II as the Council of the Church, bespeaks an obligation in our life and also calls for stress in the practical order.

The Council was less doctrinal than pastoral in nature, in the sense that it sought to transform the life of the Church's members — in the sense that the doctrinal patrimony which it expounded is to nourish souls for the Church's renewal.

Precisely in a spirit of submission to this pastoral exhortation of the Council, we have tried to stress the ecclesial concept of the religious life as characteristic of our renewal, whether as individuals or as an institute.

The ecclesial view of the religious life has clearly practical consequences. Not remaining at the doctrinal level, the light and ardor of this view transform themselves into strength. This light, this ardor, this strength must become life.

The program of our entire religious life may be summed up in this statement: *for me to live is the Church;* that is, in my life I must express the doctrine and reality of the Mystical Body of Christ, which is the Church.

We are in the spirit of St. Paul, in the spirit of his: *"for me to live is Christ."* He lived Christ as Head of the Church, as Master and Priest in and for the Church.

This motto: "For me to live is the Church" is illuminated and implemented in diverse communities and situations, yet the fact remains that each religious is to live the Church, as the Church is manifested through the religious' own institute.

70

PRIESTLY LIFE

Religious profession involves a communication of personality. Through it the novice gives himself to the Church and the Church gives herself to him. The Church places each religious upon the altar; thus, the religious should consider himself as remaining continuously on the altar as victim and priest.

To be sure, the Church stresses the sacrificial aspect of the religious, but the Mass is such that its victim is its priest and its priest is its victim; in profession the Church unites us with Jesus the Victim and Jesus the Priest, and we remain on the altar continuously.

There is no other life as liturgical as the religious life, precisely because we place ourselves in a continuous state of worshiping, in the Church, through the Church, and in the name of the Church.

Let us religious enter into the liturgical movement with our whole life, for our life is a continuous liturgy. Ours is a *liturgical state;* the liturgy is the exercise of the virtue of religion. To be sure, all Christians and all priests must practice the virtue of religion, but the word "religious," used as a noun and not merely as an adjective, was coined precisely to designate the status of one who has made profession of the evangelical counsels. Religion places us in a status of worshiper; the religious is always on the altar as priest and victim, like Jesus, with Jesus and in Jesus.

We must recall that our prayer, spiritual reading and discussions are aimed at making us review our life in the light of conciliar doctrine in order to heal whatever is defective, wanting or incomplete in us. They should correct and improve us; they should provide some new element which, when incorporated into our spiritual organism, will enable us to act, live and work in conformity with the Council, and to renew and convert ourselves.

LIFE OF IMMOLATION

From the foregoing we deduce other points and practical considerations. An ecclesial vision of ourselves should make us come out of our "little ego." So often our life is vitiated by the preoccupation of asserting ourselves, of placing ourselves — our being and our actions — at the center of everything. Such an attitude contrasts radically with that of the priest-victim. By their very nature, priest and victim serve not themselves but God, and others for God.

If my personality matters, it matters only insofar as it is given for the glory of God and the service of my brethren.

So much is said these days, of respect for personality, adult character and fulfillment. All this is good if viewed in the light of the Gospel: "He who loves his life, loses it; and he who hates his life in this world, keeps it unto life everlasting," or: "Unless the grain of wheat falls into the ground and dies, it remains alone. But if it dies it brings forth much fruit" (Jn. 12:24-25).

Nowadays it is easy to forget or ignore the fact that the paschal mystery consists not only in the phase of resurrection, but also in the phase of passion. The paschal mystery is not solely the joy and glory of the resurrection; it is rooted in Calvary, in the humiliation of the cross.

Between the joyful and glorious mysteries of the rosary, come the sorrowful mysteries, which lead from joy to glory.

It is easy to set the passion aside. However, we cannot change the paschal mystery. In the paschal mystery, relived in us as the Church, there must also be a passion through the immolation of our ego.

Yes, living the life of the Church obliges us to come out of ourselves, yet at the same time it lifts us on high, raising our hearts to God. I must not seek my glory, my success, my advantage, my gain. Such an attitude would be fundamentally opposed to an ecclesial personality, which exhorts us to make the Church's interests our own.

FRUITFUL LIFE

The vows should be understood in this ecclesial perspective.

Poverty impels us to go beyond detachment from natural goods; it helps us to understand that we should not yield to expediency, however spiritual, in our religious life. Chastity frees and opens the heart. It liberates the heart from attractions and antipathies and opens it to all, enlarging it in response to everyone's needs.

It is not simply the renunciation of matrimony that prevails in chastity, but a characteristic wholeness of heart—a heart which opens itself to God and in God to one's neighbor—a wholeness filled with sensitivity and love toward all. Chastity is the charity of the Church; it is the love of the Church, who is virgin and mother that she may be able to embrace all.

This ecclesial awareness makes us sensitive, conscientious, charitable and motherly toward all; it obliges us to emerge from the confines of self and our own environment. The encyclical "On Holy Virginity" presents chastity to us as a sharing in the maternity of the Church.

Moreover, the ecclesial perspective gives us the true sense of obedience and renders us obedient. Our dependence upon the superior is not a duty imposed from without. It is not an imprisonment of ourselves as a result of an extrinsic bond, but it is the full development of the self living in the Church. It is this living in and of the Church which keeps the religious in contact with authority. Therefore, far from being a limitation and a fetter, obedience is a source of liberty, a wellspring of life.

In *Lumen Gentium*, n. 46, it may be clearly seen that those who are more closely bound to the Church have a stronger personality, and that in the Church they reach full maturity.

There is a beautiful passage of St. Augustine which states that we are, as it were, contained in the bosom of the Church, who forms and molds us so as to be able to generate and mature us for eternal life. This expression of St. Augustine, which St. Louis de Montfort applied to the Mother of God, shows us our position in relation to the Church. The Church purifies us, helps us to correct ourselves, gives us a charitable outlook and places us in an attitude of availability for others. A member of a body is at the disposition of the entire body, and, living in the organism, it contributes to the good of all. *Availability, service* and *immolation* with regard to others—perhaps we demand all these of others, yet do not always have such dispositions ourselves.

The ecclesial perspective of the religious life conveys a new outlook and sheds new light, both in the evaluation of things in order to accept or reject them and in the facing of the situation; it lifts us above many trifles.

LIFE OF RESPONSIBILITY

An ecclesial orientatation also aids in understanding the work and responsibility of authority, which is a position of serving the Church and leading to her life.

The superior is called upon to direct the community in the name of the Church, to communicate the life of the Church to those entrusted to him, and to simultaneously incorporate these individuals into the life of the Church. Could there be a more sublime and more profound view of the role of authority and of the responsibility attached to this service—which is an ecclesial service?

Authority communicates the life of the Church, leads to the life of the Church, and binds to the Church; hence it is not a reward but a service, a duty, an obligation, a particular submission to the Church.

Authority is obedience, availability and docility to the Church; it is the immolation of self to the Church. The Church calls upon us to serve her more completely; authority is obedience to the Church.

The very rights of authority are sources of duties: duties toward the Church and toward one's brethren. One certainly does not have the right to decide and do what he wants. The rights of one's brothers are the duties of authority, and the first duty is to obey the Church. Superiors only have duties—duties which give them the authority to be obeyed.

The first duty of authority is the sense of service. Our Lady gives us an example of this. Having been chosen to become the Mother of God, she did not reflect upon the lofty position she could attain, but exclaimed at once: "Behold the handmaid of the Lord" (Lk. 1:38). Voluntarily and spontaneously the handmaid declared her position of utter dependence.

From the moment in which Mary was called to be Mother of God, she was also called to be queen. She confronted this dignity with utter dependence, and became the mother of sorrows and queen of martyrs.

Submission and humility oppose neither activity nor authority, for while we divest ourselves of everything which could be pure personalism, submission and humility give us a fuller capacity to participate in the life of the Church, which is a life of development, dynamism and fervor.

LIFE OF SERVICE

This ecclesial outlook is reflected in community life, prayer life and mortification. Our whole life should be given an ecclesial orientation. Thus, everything can be linked up with the life of the Church, so that it takes our whole being — in every moment, expression and situation — and unites it to the entire life of the Church, which we should digest, absorb, assimilate and foster according to our vocation. This is the meaning which we should give to the conciliar expression "in accordance with their own characteristics." Our entire life should enter into the life of the Church, and the entire life of the Church should enter into our life.

This integration obliges us to know the whole life of the Church, as set forth by the Council, since all of it has close bearing on us.

Thus fully integrated into the life of the Church, we are integrated into the life of the world with and through the Church. That is why the "Constitution on the Church in the Modern World" has such importance for us.

Our integration into the Church opens us up to the whole world and keeps us always on the altar. But our altar is located in the world, and we must render the Church present upon it with our priestly and consecrated life, in accord with our institute's special character.

At the very moment that Jesus came within her, the Blessed Virgin felt herself to be the mother of all and incorporated into the plan of God. She felt that she belonged to the world, and she went at once to her cousin Elizabeth, to communicate her Son to her, and in Elizabeth to all.

Let us ask Mary to obtain for us the grace of an ecclesial personality more marked, full and active, more open to all the world.

CHAPTER 11

LIVING AND THINKING
WITH THE CHURCH IN ORDER
TO SERVE HER IN HER MISSION

The "Decree on Priestly Training" states that clerics should be imbued with the mystery of the Church, and *Perfectae Caritatis*, n. 6, declares that we must participate in the Church's life ever more intensely:

"Living and thinking ever more in union with the Church, (they will) dedicate themselves wholly to its mission."

"The Decree on the Ministry and Life of Priests," n. 14, states that the bond with the Church and with Christ is the principal unifying influence in the priestly life, which can be distracted by so many occupations, duties, demands and necessities:

"Priests will find the coordination and unity of their own life in the oneness of the Church's mission. They will be joined with the Lord and through Him with the Father in the Holy Spirit. This will bring them great satisfaction and a full measure of happiness."

Precisely in this strong bond with the Church priests and religious find the coordinating theme for their whole existence, the source which harmonizes and unifies their multiplicity of activities. Fidelity to Christ cannot be divorced from fidelity to His Church.

Let us continue to examine the conciliar texts, in order to immerse ourselves ever more deeply in the mystery of the Church. After these considerations we should be changed and renewed to some extent, so that the Church may be our life. In studying the documents we should be attentive, exact and penetrating, making them the leaven of our lives, as it were, and grounding ourselves ever more firmly in the truth: "For me to live is the Church."

ACCORDING TO THEIR OWN CHARACTERISTICS

As we have said, *Perfectae Caritatis,* n. 6, recalls institutes to the duty of living and thinking always more intensely with the Church and of dedicating themselves to her mission *in accordance with their own characteristics.* This italicized phrase is very important, especially these days. Today there is enthusiasm for either a little of everything or for a certain type or method of apostolate only. The good at the root of all this is not enough. Order and capability are needed. Each must remain at his own post, for the Church is an organism, a society, where not all hold the same position and not all have the same duty, mission and vocation.

Both as an institute and as a member thereof, we must remain at our proper post—the post which the Church has designated.

The type of work and purpose of an institute are not merely the result of the founder's personal design as actualized by the first religious; they have the sanction of the Church. If some retouching is needed, therefore, this should be done according to the Church's guidelines and always in accord with the institute's own characteristics.

WITH KNOWING HARMONY

Undoubtedly there could be some change or adaptation in activity or in manner of working. However, once a position has been assigned, this is the position in which we must live, whether as an institute or as an individual.

There are religious of good will who would like to work in undertakings allowed by the institute, but which are their own desires. Not all the members of an organism can have the same function.

The institute is *an ecclesial state, a miniature Church,* and, therefore, it is an organism. Various sectors may also be distinguished within the institute, and it is within these sectors, by doing whatever has been assigned to us, that we share in the good of the Church.

Even the smallest labor out among the souls, in the kitchen or at the doorkeeper's post, makes us part of the vital and dynamic flux of the Church, according to God's plan.

Thus, by accepting everything God sends us and asks of us, and by corresponding well, we will be right where He has willed us to be.

If the Lord wishes us to remain in a certain position, let us do all the good we can in it, with an ecclesial awareness. In this way we will bring about our union with the Church, for we are there where the Church has placed us.

The more we live where the Church has placed us, the more we live of the Church.

Our every initiative, our every contribution of mind or heart, should pass through the Church. Let us draw strength and energy from the wellspring of the Church.

WITHIN THE CONTEXT OF DIRECTIVES

In accordance with their own characteristics, states the decree. Fidelity in remaining at our proper post does not estrange us from other sectors of the Church. Remaining at our post, we live the whole life of the Church, and the whole life of the Church flows through us. Everything contributes to the life of the Church, and we collaborate for the good of the Church in the spot where she has placed us.

Each little wheel turning in synchronization with others exerts an influence upon the entire mechanism; it receives and gives. But if, instead, it runs on its own, it accomplishes nothing. The same thing happens when one takes many steps, but away from the road; the steps serve for nothing.

Right now, in a spirit of initiative and humility, every institute should see, examine, inspect and ask itself whether, perhaps, the Church is asking it to make some adjustment in its choices of action, or to change a way of working, or to update a method. If not, the institute will obey by remaining at its own post. Fidelity to the institute is not the stiff and static fidelity of a museum, but a dynamic fidelity.

> States *Perfectae Caritatis*, n. 2c:
> "All institutes should share in the life of the Church, adapting as their own and implementing in accordance with their own characteristics the Church's undertakings and aims in matters biblical, liturgical, dogmatic, pastoral, ecumenical, missionary and social."

This enumeration is one of exemplification. It is neither all-embracing, nor final, nor exhaustive. There are many other initiatives which the Church has promoted and which ought to be promoted!

How can we undertake certain activities — social or political, for instance? If we consider each of these initiatives and measure it against the characteristics of the institute, we may be greatly illuminated. However, everything must be seen within its own frame of reference or environment, and in any case, aggiornamento and adaptation should always be made in accord with the Church's directives. Someone might say: "I am free to do what I want." Agreed. Free as a person, yes; but as a religious, no. We must be at the command of the Church, for we belong to the Church. We are not the supreme authority, and we are not free to do whatever we wish.

IN HARMONY WITH THE CHURCH

For good or evil, our conduct exerts an influence upon the Church, and our participation in the life of the Church should be practical in order to be vital.

The biblical movement. The Gospel is to be the supreme rule of the religious life. The norms implementing the conciliar decree call for the fostering of its study from the time of the novitiate on. As religious, we should have the Sacred Scriptures in our hands daily.

Therefore, the study of the Gospel should be part of the program of formation followed in the novitiate and the juniorate. It is necessary to lead the young to understand and savor Sacred Scripture, always doing so in response to the demands of the special character of the institute.

The liturgical movement. This presents no difficulty. The "Constitution on the Sacred Liturgy" sets forth what the Church asks of religious, and *Perfectae Caritatis*, n. 6, notes that we should nourish ourselves with the liturgy, the richest font of the spiritual life.

The norms for the implementation of *Perfectae Caritatis* (*Ecclesiae Sanctae*, n. 20) commend this proposal when speaking of the recitation of the Divine Office, in whole or in part: "so that (the religious) may participate more intimately in the liturgical life of the Church."

Ecclesiae Sanctae, n. 21, recommends giving a larger place to mental prayer, so that religious may participate always more intimately and fruitfully in the most holy mystery of the Eucharist and the public prayer of the Church, and that their whole spiritual life may be nourished more abundantly.

According to the "Constitution on the Sacred Liturgy," n. 98, all religious who recite the Divine Office and even the "Little Office" are praying in the name of the Church. Their voice is the voice of the Church.

Such a declaration is an exhortation to adaptation, and could suggest some suitable innovations to be studied in the chapters. But it is the will of the Church that the practices of piety commonly in use be respected. Furthermore, it should be kept in mind that the liturgy does not exhaust all the activity of the Church, and that, therefore, the liturgical movement does not mean the setting aside of all else. We can and *we must* conserve whatever constitutes our own spirituality, such as those exercises which are distinctive and yet in conformity with the laws and norms of the Church. Among the prayers to be conserved, the Holy Father recommends the rosary, which has an eminently biblical content, as a resumé of the whole of salvation history. This is the reply to those who have wanted to replace the rosary with a Bible vigil; the latter is an undeniably beautiful practice, but it detracts not at all from the beauty of the holy rosary. The rosary is not a withered leaf which should drop off to give place to others.

Although we are called upon to nourish ourselves by means of the liturgy, we need not be inclined to discard everything else. The liturgy does have its voice, but the Church does not have this voice alone; she also expresses herself and prays with other voices in other ways.

The liturgical criterion must not be an absolute standard; otherwise, we would be saying good-by to the rosary, way of the cross, particular examen, eucharistic visit, benediction and other eucharistic devotions.

Thus, certain practices proper to the institute are not to be discarded immediately and *en bloc*. The Council has been wise and balanced, knowing how it should proceed and knowing how to point out the most suitable path for us. If all depended upon certain absolute liturgists, the liturgy would vanish.

The dogmatic-doctrinal movement. This movement obliges us, and must be followed. It has already been entered upon with the institution of the juniorate — with a more in-depth plan of study for the formation of members — as is elsewhere called for in *Perfectae Caritatis*, n. 18.

In more detail, the implementing norms, *Ecclesiae Sanctae*, set forth the necessity of institutes' attending to the renewal of their religious life through the study of Sacred Scripture and religious doctrine in its theological, historical, canonical and social aspects.

Whose task is it to explain this religious doctrine?

Certainly it is the task of superiors who must shoulder this new burden. Hence, the importance of penetrating and possessing this doctrine oneself. Moreover, there is the spirit of the institute to be studied; this study is to be more precise, more doctrinal and more dogmatic.

The pastoral movement. In two articles of the "Decree on the Pastoral Office of Bishops in the Church," religious also are presented as cooperators of the bishop. Without wishing to comment on this, we say only that religious practice Catholic action, performing an apostolate associated with the hierarchy and are in the vanguard of the pastoral movement.

The ecumenical movement. Here, too, we have something to do. We must know this movement and be able to speak about it. We must pray for this.

It is not unusual for people to have rather vague ideas about ecumenism and its true nature. Ecumenism does not mean a federation of churches or a convergence of various churches to one sole point—not at all. The Catholic Church is not on a par with other churches; she is the *sole true*, the one true Church, even though other confessions contain some elements of truth.

This movement, too, should concern us. If we are sensitive to the desires of the heart of Jesus, we cannot let ourselves be indifferent to the urgency of: "that they may be one" (Jn. 17:11).

The missionary movement. How many teachings are to be found in the "Decree on the Mission Activity of the Church" in particular, and in the "Decree on the Apostolate of the Laity"! We should deepen our study of them and draw light and strength from them.

Another luminous document is the "Pastoral Constitution on the Church in the Modern World," which summons us to *social orientation.* In many areas the Church is rendered present by religious, rather than priests, for religious can enter into surroundings closed to priests, into places and spheres of activity not entirely ecclesiastical: assistance to the sick, education, instruction...all sectors in which the Church encounters society and into which she can infuse Christ's message to mankind.

We should understand the social movement in a broad sense. Horizons not offered to priests are open to our action as religious.

The religious is the Church. The social field is a difficult one, for which the religious needs to be formed. He needs social culture, perhaps more so than the priest, since the latter approaches his brothers on the ground of religion, whereas the religious finds himself exercising his ministry, which is an ecclesial ministry, under particular conditions.

The religious habit is not a mere uniform; it is an *ecclesial habit,* and speaks a language of its own. It declares that the religious is presenting himself in the name of the Church.

Great horizons open before the gaze of the religious. *Where the Church is, there is the religious, and where the religious is, there is the Church.*

There is no separation between the religious and the Church. The Church fuses her social mission with the religious mission; if it were otherwise, a truly dangerous and injurious dichotomy would exist. The religious presents the Church in her social mission.

CHAPTER 12

THE CHURCH MUST INCARNATE
HERSELF IN TODAY'S WORLD

While meditating and planning our individual renewal, it is profitable and very important to consider, as we have done, the principles and norms of renewal itself.

It has been said that renewing ourselves means living all the requirements of our religious vocation to the full. We renew ourselves when we place ourselves in step with the vocation God has lavished upon us. The vocation is a gift which the Lord has bestowed, in view of the Church and for the Church. The Council solemnly affirmed this fact and repeated this affirmation at various times and in various places.

HERE-AND-NOW DIMENSION

Linked to this concept is the principle set forth in *Perfectae Caritatis*, n. 2c. Our vocation has a special status in the Church, the Mystical Body of Christ, by which *we should live the life of the Church today*, uniting our religious life with that of the Church herself.

Stressing communion with the life of the Church—and the life of the Church of today—*Perfectae Caritatis*, n. 2d, observes that the life of society converges toward the Church.

This is true. The developing life of the Church does not parallel that of society, but moves toward it, while the life of society moves toward the Church.

The world and the Church are not two parallel streets, but on the contrary, two convergent lines, in the sense that the Church must incarnate herself in the world of today.

EXISTENTIAL DIMENSION

The Church exists and works, but not as a consummate reality, which has already reached its perfection. The Church must continually actualize herself in the society of every time and place, and the religious is the instrument which effects this ecclesial reality. The religious shares in the vocation and mission of the Church in the contemporary world. Through Jesus Christ and the Church, the religious is linked to the world of today, to his brethren.

Let us again hearken to the decree *Perfectae Caritatis:* "Institutes should promote among their members an adequate *knowledge of the social conditions of the times they live in and of the needs of the Church.* In such a way, judging current events wisely in the light of faith and burning with apostolic zeal, they may be able to assist men more effectively" (n. 2d).

"Members of each institute should recall first of all that by professing the evangelical counsels they responded to a divine call...to live for God alone. *They have dedicated their entire lives to His service....* Since the Church has accepted their surrender of *self they should realize they are also dedicated to its service* (n. 5).

This service is described as making us participate in the life of the Church in all its content and in all its dimensions, whether in the vertical dimension, towards God (contemplation), or in the horizontal (apostolic) dimension.

VERTICAL DIMENSION

The apostolic dimension of the Church, and hence of the religious life, stems from the contemplative life. The service which we must render to the Church is a service of divine worship, of donation to God in a life of obscurity, holiness and immolation, but it is, moreover—in virtue of

our own sharing in the Church's life of divine worship and
holiness—a service which requires our participation in her
apostolic mission, in her thrust toward the world, in her
yearnings and work of salvation. Apostolic service, therefore, is the logical consequence of the service of holiness,
and collaboration in the work of redemption is the result of
adhesion to God.

We meet this concept again in *Perfectae Caritatis*, n. 6,
where it is stated:

"Let those who make profession of the evangelical
counsels seek and love above all else God who has
first loved us and *let them strive to foster in all circumstances a life hidden with Christ in God.* This
love of God both excites and energizes the love of
one's neighbor."

HORIZONTAL DIMENSION

The service which the religious is called upon to render the Church is a service of contemplation and of zeal for
apostolic activity—an apostolic service which is a consequence and reflection of love for God, just as love for one's
neighbor is.

This is a solid, substantial, genuine doctrine, which has
to be understood in order to put our religious life in its
proper place and to live it in accord with the exigencies of
the day.

Fidelity to vocation, which includes apostolic service,
requires that institutes know the environment in which
they are to perform their apostolate—and that they know
people and their needs. Institutes and their members are to
evaluate conditions, circumstances and needs of the Church
according to the norms of faith, and *present themselves to
the world with apostolic zeal,* so as to benefit their neighbor, and the Church in their neighbor, in the most efficient
way.

Apostolic service should be the fruit of contemplation,
a reflection of the service of holiness. Insofar as we are
present in the Church with our holiness, to that extent do
we serve the Church in apostolic endeavor. In other words,

we present ourselves to our neighbor and help him, to the degree that we share in the holiness of the Church.

There is no place for egoism.

INTEGRAL DIMENSION

The position of the religious calls upon us to take stock of existing circumstances, evaluating them in the light of faith. Our vision of the present needs of the world should be illumined by the light emanating from God, from Christ, from the Church.

We present ourselves to the world as Paul VI presented himself before the United Nations: he went, not as an equal, as someone who has his own economic program, but as the Vicar of Christ bringing the message of God.

Economic, peace and social problems are evaluated in the light radiating from God and the Gospel: this is the distinctive way in which the envoy and representative of the Church presents himself.

The outlook with which we approach the problems of humanity is different from, but not opposed to, the outlook of those who examine those problems in the light of right reason, for right reason comes from God.

The religious weighs matters with a standard different from that of a professional man or sociologist; likewise, his judgment and the spirit with which he studies and confronts contemporary problems are different. The religious does these things *burning with apostolic zeal;* that is, with the objective of giving God and of bringing others to God. "What I have, that I give you. In the name of Jesus Christ of Nazareth, arise and walk," said Peter to the cripple who asked for alms beside the gate called the Beautiful (Acts 3:6). Pope Paul VI had the same attitude during his visit to the United Nations. *We, too, give the fruit which comes from Jesus.*

With this outlook, with this sharing in the mind and heart of the Church, we are in a position to carry out the Church's mission, which is to give Christ to souls and souls to Christ, as an expression of our life hidden with Christ in God. A life hidden, yes, but not enclosed—a life communicating the saving power of God, and presenting itself to the world, not with the power of money, nor with human might, nor with the promise of earthly goods, but *with the prospect and promise of an eternal good,* of everlasting joy, a promise which can even facilitate material prosperity.

We must avoid giving the impression that we religious are not concerned with material needs. We feel them, and we judge them under the light of God; we take intense interest in them, but from a particular vantage point.

This principle easily finds its application in our work among the sick, infants and the poor. Religious are the initiators of much prosperity and many beneficent institutions; they enrich humanity with many good things. But *all this is rooted in a supernatural vision,* as is expressed by the Church whose function it is to be mother of charity.

The life of holiness translates itself into apostolic zeal, by which religious are dispensers of the mysteries of God, ministers of the divine riches, which also produce social advantages.

It may thus be understood how charity toward one's neighbor springs forth from a life hidden with Christ in God. Every religious life should have its complete dimension. An apostolic dimension is no longer apostolic if it is not rooted in a life hidden with Christ in God.

HARMONIOUS DIMENSION

The "Decree on the Mission Activity of the Church" notes that every mission should be considered against the background of that mission for which the Word was sent upon the earth. Our apostolate is the reflection of this divine life precisely because it is hidden with Christ in God.

The more our apostolate expresses the service of holiness, the more effective it will be.

The renewal of the religious life, insofar as it is apostolic, should have this light and orientation of interiority, of interior richness, of contemplation. Apostolate and holiness are not two parallel lines. The apostolate should be the continuation of contemplation. Neither apostolate nor contemplation holds priority or second place. We are religious and apostles. Ours is a religious life with an apostolic outlook and overflow. We are at once religious and apostles inasmuch as our apostolate is the fruit of our religious life.

Our clinging to God generates love of neighbor. The religious apostolic life denotes *apostolic religious and religious apostles*. There is an absolute unity. Let us thus understand that our religious life is to be renewed by underlining the theological, Christological and ecclesial aspects of our apostolate, for unless apostolate is the expression of a life hidden with Christ in God, it is beneficent activity, but not apostolate.

Mary most holy is united to her neighbor because she is united to God. She is our mother inasmuch as she is the Mother of Jesus. Her tie with us results from her bond with Jesus.

This reality calls for renewal in our concepts and thoughts: our apostolate is an expression of the service of holiness and is a consequence thereof.

CHAPTER 13

SPIRITUAL RENEWAL,
THE SOUL OF AGGIORNAMENTO

We need the light and strength which come to us from the Holy Spirit, the spirit of truth and fortitude; we need the help of the holy Virgin, in order to meditate on another principle of aggiornamento as presented to us by the Council. This fifth principle should be grasped, weighed and applied well, that it may help us properly to situate ourselves in the life of the Church and in the attitude most fitting for us in our renewal and adaptation of religious life.

In this historic moment in the life of the Church, in this hour of God who expects our fidelity, it is important to have a clear idea of the renewal and adaptation of the religious life of both the institute and individual members. This principle clarifies what has already been said:

"The purpose of the religious life is to help the members follow Christ and be united to God through the profession of the evangelical counsels. It should be constantly kept in mind, therefore, that even the best adjustments made in accordance with the needs of our age will be ineffectual unless they are animated by a renewal of spirit. This must take precedence over even the active ministry" *(Perfectae Caritatis*, n. 2e).

EXACT EVALUATION

These conciliar statements thus recall and motivate the affirmation that the religious life is: first and foremost a

90

following of Christ; a union with Christ in the evangelical counsels in particular; a theological, Christocentric life, ordered to Christ in a special way. It is important to remember all this now that we are called upon to look round about us, to open our eyes to ourselves and to the world for an adjustment to the requirements of time and place. In this opening up, in this updating, there can be the risk of forgetting the fundamental and of remaining a little confused in the face of the coexisting absolute and relative; it could happen that the sight of the world would somewhat obscure our vision.

The Council points out that we should place ourselves in the proper position to have an exact view of the world. This view will be given by our religious life, as a clinging to Christ, as the following of Christ through the observance of the holy vows.

This is the viewpoint from which we must look upon the world in order to evaluate present needs with accuracy and respond to them with serenity and balance.

Perhaps this is the number of *Perfectae Caritatis* in which the *two components of aggiornamento,* renewal and adaptation, are most clearly distinguished from one another; they are placed one before the other, so that the rapport and relation between them may easily be seen.

This paragraph of the decree is intended to form in us a mentality by which we will view the world and circumstances as religious, that is, as persons who have anchored themselves in God and have made Him the object of their affections, desires, occupations and preoccupations; thus, we will present ourselves to the world with the attitudes of Jesus Christ Himself.

COMPLEMENTARITY

Aggiornamento will not succeed unless it is the fruit of spiritual renewal.

The conciliar decree furthermore restates the problem of relationships between the interior life and the life of the apostolate, between the content of the religious life as such and the content of the apostolic life. They are not two opposite poles, but complements. Nonetheless, it is necessary that there be a clear vision of the relative positions of renewal and adaptation, of interior life and apostolic life.

Above all, renewal dictates a return to the fonts of the spiritual life, with which it is concerned, and demands an intensification of the spiritual life as viewed in the concrete, in the present renewal movement. Renewal thus calls for the acceptance of a life of constant, continuous, ceaseless adhesion to Jesus Christ; a life hidden with Christ in God; a religious life which is fuller and with a higher concentration of supernatural meaning, more dynamic, as modern times require.

The necessary adaptation will be derived precisely from the religious life lived intensely, dynamically and fully, as it emanates from Jesus Christ, just as service to the Church in the apostolic dimension arises from the life of consecration to God and service to the Church in the contemplative dimension. As we have said before, and here repeat, interior life and apostolate do not oppose one another, nor are they two lines placed side by side which then diverge and go off on their own. Rather, the end of the one is the beginning of the other; renewal is the basis of adaptation. The apostolate must be born of the interior life; that is, the apostolate must be the flower and fruit of the interior life.

A religious life which is profoundly experienced and faithfully lived will discern the will of God—the signs of God in persons, activities, and circumstances, so as to encounter Him and bind itself to Him ever more tightly.

The religious life is not afraid of adaptation, but rather seeks it, for the beam of light guiding the religious life to God is lit precisely through adaptation.

Interior life and apostolate, interior life and exterior activity, should flow full force from religious life. Adaptation can never imply a religious life which is less religious; it can never justify a diminution of the religious life, understood as a life of union with Jesus, of following Jesus, of exclusive adhesion to Him. Any adaptation which would place limits on this wholehearted following of Christ and intimacy with Him, absolutely should not be accepted.

It is necessary to distinguish between the substantial religious life and those exercises or practices which somewhat resemble the riverbanks or streambed through which the religious life flows.

RENEWAL OF SPIRIT

Adaptation can call for some change, but this will always be in regard to details of its margins, of the riverbed. There might indeed be some reduction or substitution in practices of piety, as there might also be some modification in penitential practices. In no wise does this imply a diminution of the spirit of prayer and penance, nor a lessening of esteem for their importance in the religious life. We must always be fired by a spirit of penance and of renunciation, never seeking after our comfort, benefit or satisfaction....

The substance must always be respected.

Sometimes we run the risk of deceiving ourselves and yielding to certain forms of adaptation under the pretext of having a more comfortable life, a watered-down religious life.

St. Francis de Sales adapted his Institute of the Visitation to the exigencies of the times and the personnel, shortening the night vigils and mitigating the harshest penances to such an extent that someone jokingly called that institute the "institute of the deposition from the cross." But the dart of irony missed its target; the saint had only made an adaptation to the place and to the physical possibilities of the religious.

The most important action in adaptation will not consist in an intense study or a multiplication of discussions. To renew itself, the institute must renew its spirit and members. It must effect the *spiritual conversion* of its members.

The norms of implementation, too, insist that renewal is primarily a renewal of spirit. The Church asks that our life hidden with Christ in God always be given the first place.

Without this interior renewal, in the sense of embracing our religious life as the *following of Christ* and as communion with Christ, all would be sterile. We have also taken this duty upon ourselves before the world.

ANCHORED IN GOD

The general orientation of the interior life is the same for all, for the vocation to holiness is only one. But the religious goes to God directly, with an undivided heart, and gives God to the world. It is true that the faithful, too, look about themselves and fashion the world into a stairway which they can climb to reach God. Using their earthly possessions and the opportunity to dispose of themselves and plan for themselves—they climb to God, and this is beautiful, good and right. However, we religious have a more distinctive characteristic; we aim directly toward God, going to Him with a heart which is undivided, whether in regard to earthly goods, affections or the planning of our life; we anchor ourselves in God, and from Him we return to persons, things and ourselves.

Religious have a particular obligation to evaluate all things under the light of God. With this supernatural vision, the delicacy and refinement of chastity are understood, as are the nature of obedience and the meaning of detachment. In a world wholly bent upon the assertion of liberty in every sector, we exercise the freedom of immolating ourselves and placing ourselves in the heart of God: "I will, O Lord, that You dispose of me, as You please. Lord, I want to do only and always Your will."

This orientation, which God has given to our life with our vocation, and which we have given with our "yes," is the basic principle of our renewal.

We should not be afraid of whatever winds blow, for we are anchored by a secure and firm base.

We should ascertain whether or not we have a clear outlook and a desire to be wholly religious, as the Lord expects us to be today. Let us leave the past alone and make an act of humility: "Lord, I want to say my total *yes* to You in this moment; I want to live my *yes* to the full, as You will it." Aggiornamento means living the *today of God*.

It is necessary that a vital communication be established with Jesus, and in Him with the Father and the Holy Spirit. And then, the Blessed Virgin well knows how to tell us what the Lord wants from us and from our institute, according to our institute's nature and special character.

Every institute should view itself as the Lord meant it to be and as He willed it to become in fact. Aggiornamento must never forget this. Thus, light and purification are needed, so that we may see ourselves in God and view our religious life as the following of Christ and the profession of the evangelical counsels.

DIVINE PREDILECTION

This question might arise in someone's mind: "But why have I become a religious?"

After making comparisons, one could draw this conclusion: "How different my life is from that of others!" Certainly, but is it better or worse? The comparison should not be made by placing the two types of life on the balance trays of the same scale, but *by considering them in the light of God's choice* and the divine plans. From this viewpoint there is no doubt that our life is better.

"Disposing of myself, I could have done so much...." Certainly, but we must relate ourselves to the call of God, to the act of predilection on the part of God, to the plan of God. Now, it is certain that the vocation is an act of infinite love, and this places me in a better and loftier position than others. The Council did not make comparisons regarding religious life; comparisons were made only when the material and the spiritual were spoken of.

Beautiful indeed the religious life will appear in the light of eternity. Great will this beacon flash appear! It is not a momentary beam which lights up and is extinguished in time; it is a beam which projects itself into eternity, into the mirror of God, into the design of God.

ADULTS OF THE MATURE AGE OF CHRIST

The religious life involves self-denial and penance; it requires a "no," so that one may say "yes" to the Lord. Having bound his own life totally to God, it is logical that the religious should have no other directions or attractions, good in themselves but not befitting a life oriented exclu-

sively, totally toward God. The religious life is a life of
liberty and of maturity. In it we truly become adults, for we
root ourselves in God and share in the maturity of Christ.
Following Christ, we absorb His thoughts, His desires,
His viewpoints and wants and we also receive light for
judging better the things of the world, for understanding,
weighing and selecting what today is requisite for adaptation to particular circumstances.

Who can think of a character more mature, more adult,
than that of Christ? In the totality of our adhesion to Him
we shall find the truest, most authentic maturity.

CHAPTER 14

THE APOSTOLATE AS A MEANS OF SPIRITUAL LIFE

While meditating on the fifth principle of renewal, we might have gathered the impression that an opposition exists between the interior life and dedication to the apostolate, or at least that it is very difficult to harmonize the two. When we thoroughly examine these elements as presented by *Perfectae Caritatis,* the impression gradually disappears.

The text states that a renewal of spirit "must take precedence over even the active ministry." Therefore, a question can arise concerning priority and second place in regard to interior renewal and the apostolate—a question which deserves to be more deeply explored and meditated.

EXPRESSION OF LOVE

Fortunately the Council solves the problem in *Perfectae Caritatis,* n. 8. Apostolic activities, in fact, do not concern adaptation alone, but enter into the first movement, that of renewal—for the apostolate and its activities form a part of the spiritual life. They are rooted in it, express it, manifest it and nourish themselves of it. The works of the apostolate are acts of the spiritual life.

In facing and exposing this problem, it is an exaggeration to present the apostolate as a danger for the spiritual life and apostolic activities as a preoccupation for the same —something to be exercised with caution.

97

Perfectae Caritatis, n. 8, gives us the key with which to solve this problem, just as other conciliar documents guide us in the preservation of harmony between the two realities, and still more in the presentation of the apostolate as a means of spiritual life.

Instead of constituting an obstacle to the love of God, love of neighbor is a proof of love for the Lord Himself. "How can he who does not love his brother, whom he sees, love God, whom he does not see?" says St. John (1 Jn. 4:20). If we do not do good works for our neighbor, how can we say we love God, who does not need our good works?

In the Gospel of the Last Sunday after Pentecost, we read that Jesus identifies Himself with the poor, the imprisoned, the naked and hungry. Herein lies the answer to our question: the activities with which we seek and encounter God in our neighbor are expressions of love for God, and they nourish themselves with this very love.

SUBSTANTIAL PART OF THE RELIGIOUS LIFE

Number 8, one of the most beautiful articles of *Perfectae Caritatis*, canonizes what we already know, even though we had never received an official pronouncement on it.

The apostolate is not a secondary and accidental element which comes along to attach itself to the life of consecration to God; it is, instead, a substantial part of this consecration to the Lord, and hence of the religious life.

It is not accurate to speak of religious life and of apostolate; it is better to speak of apostolic religious life, or religious life which leads to and denotes apostolate.

The Church is not a body in which all have the same function. It is a body in which there are many functions, for which each has his gift, according to the grace he has been given. One has the gift of ministry, another teaches, another exhorts, another dispenses with liberality, another carries out works of mercy cheerfully. There is a variety of charisms, but the Spirit is the same.

Institutes founded to help others and to educate have apostolic and charitable activity as a substantial element in their religious life. Therefore, teaching, parochial activities, help to orphans, and so forth, are not merely undertakings entrusted to them so that they may accomplish something in the Church; rather, these constitute a part of their life, as a substantial element. Theirs is thus an ecclesial service whether in contemplating, or in caring for the sick, aiding the poor, educating, and so forth.

In virtue of her mission, the Church has two dimensions: contemplative and charitable. Apostolic service is on a direct line with contemplative service; both of them are expressions of the one love for God.

Every religious institute must be apostolic, even if each has its specific duty. Let us remember the apostolic constitution *Sponsa Christi*, in which it was made clear that even the way of life of cloistered nuns has its apostolic dimension, since every religious institute in the Church—exactly because it is religious—must be apostolic.

IN THE NAME OF THE CHURCH

This statement has its special beauty and its obligation. Apostolic and charitable action constitute a sacred ministry, which must be exercised in the name of the Church. This is to say: "For us to live is the Church."

Therefore, the religious finds himself committed to the apostolate as to a sacred ministry. Following a profession, we exercise it not with a professional right, but with a title of sacred ministry entrusted to us by the Church and carried out in her name. The Church receives our offering with our religious profession, makes it hers and communicates to us her personality—her maternal character—in charitable activity. Charity is part of the function of the Church, and it is beautiful to see that women especially, with their sensitivity, are invested by the Church with her charitable role, in the carrying out of her works of mercy.

Since the Church is mother, she also has the function of charity, by means of her help, beneficence and all the undertakings with which she expresses her goodness.

ECCLESIAL DIACONATE

Lumen Gentium, n. 8, focuses our attention on the mystery in which the Church encompasses with loving care those who are afflicted with human weakness; recognizing in the poor and suffering the image of her poor and suffering Founder, the Church is solicitous to relieve their needs and to serve, in them, Christ Himself.

Who else, though not a deacon, can best express the diaconate? Ninety-nine percent of those who develop this ecclesial ministry of charity are sisters who have been invested with this ministry by the Church. It is primarily in her religious women that we find the Church acting as servant and as deacon.

Let us also examine the "Decree on Priestly Training," which is very important and useful to religious, since the spiritual life of him who is in the Church is invested with a ministerial mission that must be endowed with interiority. The Church repeats that the priest must sanctify himself through his ministry. And we must sanctify ourselves through the ministry of the works of spiritual and material help. However, this is not a sacrament which sanctifies by itself, without need of other means. Religious must find God in themselves; they must acquire familiarity with the Lord with whom they come in contact through prayer and mortification. Finding God in ourselves, we shall be able to bring Him to our neighbor and to bring our neighbor to God.

UNIQUE FLAME OF CHARITY

The apostolate, therefore, is not opposed to holiness. Nonetheless, given our nature and our proclivity to go after external things and stop at them, we cannot rule out the danger that in seeking the poor we will stop at the poor, and that in seeking the needy and the sick we will stop when we have reached them. In that case, our seeking would not have been done in the name of the Lord. The danger does exist, and it is because of this that we must have a strong, dynamic spiritual life, which will animate the activities of our apostolate and bring souls and ourselves to God through these same endeavors.

Thus, activities are again to be found among the means of sanctification. If we are well equipped spiritually, we shall find Christ in our neighbor, and our holiness will express itself in the apostolate, through which it will be seen clearly, as is stated in *Perfectae Caritatis*, n. 8:

"The whole religious life of (the institutes') members should be inspired by an apostolic spirit and all their apostolic activity animated by the spirit of religion."

Therefore, there is a *complete compenetration* between the two aspects of the religious life. They are like two rays of light: one emanates from the consecration of oneself to God, and the other from the urge to bring God to one's brethren; yet both constitute one sole flame of charity.

Our spirituality is that in which *the spiritualities of consecration to God and dedication to one's neighbor converge.*

Our spiritual life should nourish itself not only upon the spirituality of contemplatives, but also upon apostolic spirituality. The "Decree on the Apostolate of the Laity" and the "Decree on the Mission Activity of the Church" also concern religious.

MEANS OF SANCTIFICATION

It is partially true that in the past, religious asceticism was connected with the life of contemplatives, who looked upon the apostolate with a certain fear. We recall the phrase of à Kempis: "Every time I go down among men, I return less a man."

Apostolic works should be a means of sanctification. The religious who returns from school or from a hospital ward, should be more of a religious when he returns than he was when he left.

But how is it possible, it will be asked, to fulfill, in certain circumstances, all our duties of apostolate and all our practices of piety? And what should be said of the sacramentalism of the apostolate, through which — as some would have it — the apostolate sanctifies of itself: "Our tabernacle is among the infants, the sick and the poor, and our way of the cross in the aisles of a hospital ward, and our spiritual reading in conversation with others!"

This is all beautiful poetry. In practice, one runs the risk of becoming blind and no longer able to see the Lord, of becoming deaf and no longer able to hear Him. There is a grave danger of smothering the life of prayer.

The apostolate is part of the spiritual life but it does not exhaust it. On the other hand, we must never consider the apostolate as if it were a diminution of the religious life or a deduction from the time consecrated to the Lord.

God wants the *proper dosage,* and this is the role of the Holy Spirit and of the authority of the Church, who tell us that activities and prayers must be harmonized in our life, and show us the wellsprings from which we should take our sustenance.

RECIPROCITY BETWEEN CONTEMPLATION AND APOSTOLATE

It can happen that adaptation may alter the dosage a little and touch upon the practices of piety to some extent. Then we must not confuse prayer with its practices, just as we must not confuse apostolate with the works of apostolate. Apostolate is not our work, but our encounter with God in our neighbor.

We must be apostles in contemplation. We exercise a greater apostolate in prayer, in a way of the cross...than when we are in contact with our fellowmen in school, in surgery, and so forth.

And we must be contemplatives in the apostolate.

The apostolate must permeate our life of contact with God, and our life of contact with God must permeate our apostolate, so that our apostolic zeal will be purified and rejuvenated, enlivened by our union with God and our union with the Church.

We are apostles when we perform a practice of piety, and we are religious when we do an act of charity.

In *Perfectae Caritatis,* n. 8, we read:

"In order that religious may first correspond to their vocation to follow Christ and serve Him in His members, their apostolic activities must spring from intimate union with Him. *Thus love itself towards God and the neighbor is fostered.*"

There are no clashes nor discords in the religious life. We travel on one road: that of consecration to God.

IN FRATERNAL COMMUNION

The apostolate does not exhaust itself in the moment in which one is teaching or assisting the sick or the poor. Our entire religious life is apostolate.

Even sick religious are apostles. Those who are in rest homes carry out an apostolate. One who works in a hospital ward or teaches in a school or is occupied in charitable works in any manner whatsoever, should not attribute success to himself. The apostolate of the community benefits not only those who are in the front lines, manning the breach, but also those who take care of the lines of supply.

This is the advantage of community life, by which all of us are always in ecclesial activity, united, jointly responsible, participating in all the activities of the institute.

Many of these reflections concerning our renewal can be made again and again.

The Blessed Mother lived the mystery of the Church to the full, and was closely united to Jesus in His contemplative and apostolic mission. We recall her example at the foot of the cross, associating herself with the most full and solemn act of the redemption, while Jesus immolated Himself.

Let us ask Mary that we may live a life at once of contemplation and apostolate for the redemption of our brethren, that like her and with her we may be associated with the redemptive work of Jesus. How many times in the conciliar texts does this concept recur—a concept of a life that is at the same time one of worship, of apostolate and of redemptive commitment.

CHAPTER 15

CONSTITUTIONS IN THE LIGHT OF THE PRINCIPLES OF AGGIORNAMENTO

We need God's assistance, that He may illuminate us. He who is light *par excellence* comes to dissolve the darkness. We need strength which will transform itself into ardor; and God is love. This meditation should be given by Him, or rather, made by Him in us and by us with Him. We also need the help of the Blessed Mother, that by the light and ardor from the hearts of Jesus and Mary we may better know ourselves and conclude this reflection with a sincere resolution to absorb the light which these hearts have shed on us and to be sensitive and docile to the strength of love which they impart to us.

The five principles and criteria of renewal that we have explained, should profoundly influence our lives and cause us to take an inventory of our renewal commitment. We must analyze our life in the light of the doctrine and teachings stemming from them.

NEW SPIRIT

The renewal willed by the Council must not be relegated to the chapters or to the superiors, but must be actualized at once in each one of us, as the Holy Father states in the motu proprio *Ecclesiae Sanctae:*

"It is necessary that religious institutes promote first of all a renewal of spirit, and then that they take care to carry out this renewal adapted to their life and discipline prudently and yet skillfully...."

Therefore, an interior and personal renewal is being treated of, before a renewal of the institute as a whole.

The Council also has pastoral purposes and preoccupations in regard to each of us religious. We should be the first ones to benefit from the Council, so that we, too, may benefit others.

Renewal depends in great part upon priests and religious, who especially should initiate this spiritual conversion within themselves.

Over the years, we may have fallen into a certain attitude of tepidity. Now the Council calls for a serious examination so as to uncover whatever should be corrected and stimulated. There is an attitude to be corrected—the attitude of him who says: "What is done, is done!" The Council wills that we rouse ourselves and exert ourselves more; all must meditate and work seriously along this line.

The Council wants us to consider what the Lord expects from us as persons; thus the Council must probe into the individual and personal life of everyone. It must enter into my existence, and animate mentality, heart and life.

There is a danger of studying the Council only for the purpose of clarifying and explaining its documents to others, without aiming to assimilate it ourselves and translate it into our life. These meditations should initiate a comparison of self with the Council, that I may emerge reformed, updated and renewed.

REVISION OF THE CONSTITUTIONS

According to the mind of the Church, the five criteria of renewal already mentioned should serve for the revision of the constitutions. It is in the light of these principles that we can endow constitutions with a new and spiritual content. It is not that the Church intends, here, to correct errors; rather, she intends to recall each institute to its primitive ideal, as it appears in the primitive rule of the institute itself.

We must vitalize our constitutions in the light of the five above mentioned principles, which must be kept in mind and set into the foundation of the entire work of formation.

The program of formation should bring us back to fidelity to the Gospel and to the spirit of the institute.

It is interesting to note that the Council has not only set forth the principles of renewal but has applied them itself. In fact, the presentation of the religious life is taken back to its source, which is the following of Christ. In *Lumen Gentium,* n. 46, we read that the religious life is to be viewed as conformity to the life which Christ chose for Himself and to which the Blessed Virgin conformed herself from the first.

One of the preparatory texts of article 46 said in part: "Let the Christian conform to that type of chaste and poor life which Christ the Lord chose for Himself and for His Mother."

The Council is solicitous that every institute remain faithful to itself, precisely for the good of the Church. Also to be noted is the conciliar solicitude to cast into relief the ecclesial aspect of the religious life. The Council has given an ecclesial setting to the religious life, and has placed the Church within this same religious life.

It is eminently true that the Council is not the work of men. The Holy Spirit has guided all its undertakings, and in such a marvelous way as to manifest His presence. Without the special assistance of the Holy Spirit, the Council would not have accomplished what it did. Everything contributed to the triumph of the Paraclete: discussions, studies, contrasts, clarifications, redraftings of schemata....

Thus was illuminated the apostolic content of the religious life, which is God's gift to the Church and to humanity.

REVISION OF LIFE

The religious life is a life eminently social, altruistic and charitable. It is a gift made to all. How much good have religious institutes accomplished in various sectors of society. However, to emphasize the apostolic content of the religious life does not imply losing sight of what is eminently religious. For the religious, God is all; God is the One served. The religious life is all and only of God.

This preoccupation of the Council also enters into the practice of individual, constitutive elements of the religious life. Thus, for example, the practice of poverty is life within the context of the poverty of Jesus, as an imitation of His life. The same may be said of the other vows and of all the other elements of the religious life. Their Christological, ecclesial, apostolic, spiritual and social content are recalled and emphasized.

Poverty, then, is illustrated under its apostolic aspect, in its solicitude to bear witness to the Church of the poor, as a condition and a means for the apostolate: "an expression highly esteemed." Poverty is not merely dependence; it is affective and effective detachment with a Christocentric orientation and in the particular spirit of the institute.

The presentation and meditation of our religious life, undertaken in the light of these principles and with the necessary readiness to assimilate them and docility to put them into practice — for they are light and strength — is able to effect our renewal.

In considering the way the Church presents these principles as factors in the renewal of the religious life, we should attain to a revision of life. Thus, we must examine ourselves — attitude and mentality, dispositions and life — and ask ourselves: "Are my actions truly a following of Christ?" The Council declares that believers and non-believers alike should read the Gospel of Christ in me. So then, do my life, actions and words truly express the Gospel? Do they show the presence of Christ in me? Can I call myself the ostensorium of Christ, the manifestation of Christ and of His Church? Am I a manifestation of my institute? Do I live for others, grounded in Christ? Does or does not my way of judging, speaking and acting express the charism which the Lord gave to my founder, and which the first religious and my many predecessors received and transmitted to me, and which I must live and transmit to others?

In order to give it, we must guard it, live it and grow in it. One must give with words, but above all with his own example. The superior is he who should precede his brothers spiritually and by his example. Thus, I will ask myself if my life is really saturated with true, authentic apostolate, since fidelity to my institute places me in a position of fidelity to the Church and therefore of fidelity to her apostolic action.

No matter what his assignment, the religious must be animated by apostolic zeal. Thus he must ask himself: "Where do I stand in regard to zeal?" This temptation may present itself: "Always for others! What about myself?" The Lord was *always for others,* and always gave Himself to all.

DETAILED REVIEW

A general examination is not enough. What is necessary is a review based on each of the elements of the religious life.

Let poverty be understood as the following of Christ, according to the manner of the institute, and as fidelity to the apostolic commitment. How do I stand with regard to the vow, the virtue, the spirit and the beatitude of evangelical poverty? Is my poverty perhaps animated more by an economic criterion of saving, than by a supernatural principle? Everything should have an evangelical spirit.

In the same way we must examine the other vows, obedience, discipline, prayer life, community life, our relations with our neighbor, our life of apostolate, and so forth—for all the expressions of the religious life should be renewed precisely in the light of the five principles laid down in n. 2 of *Perfectae Caritatis:* fidelity to the Gospel, fidelity to the founder's ideal, vital bond with the Church, apostolic zeal and primacy of the spiritual life.

May the hearts of Jesus and Mary help us treasure these realities and assimilate them into life. Then there will be a spirit of simplicity, of abandonment and of trust in the Lord. Then we shall be meek, humble and serene; we shall work with the certainty that the Lord is at work within us.

CHAPTER 16

AGGIORNAMENTO AS
RESPONSE TO A LAW

The temptation to prolong a little the meditation on motives already set forth would be a good inspiration. Since we are already deeply engaged in the dynamics of renewal, it would be quite useful for a more fruitful renewal to consider the individual elements of the religious life. It would be profitable to use these in examining our whole life and that of the institute, keeping in mind the particular needs of our times.

Therefore, since renewal expresses itself in adaptation, it is necessary to consider adaptation also; this is treated in articles 3 and 4 of *Perfectae Caritatis* and to some extent in all the other articles.

GRADUAL EVOLUTION

Before commencing this study, it is necessary to note that the movement undertaken by the Council does not place the religious life in a general state of accusation. Some have chosen to interpret this movement as a reawakening from lethargy. Thus is given the impression of calling into court whatever was done in the past, as if everything had been faulty and out of place, and had to be put on trial. According to this viewpoint everything becomes uncertain.

This view and outlook are completely false. We can point out that every institute in the Church's history was always a proof and expression of aggiornamento, representing one of the most eloquent and clear signs of the Church's youthfulness. The Church keeps updated precisely through the religious life.

Here let us especially examine the history of feminine religious institutes. It reflects this development. The first Christian virgins, the rise of monasticism, the appearance, with St. Angela Merici, of souls consecrated to God and the apostolate, the uplifting of womankind which was begun precisely through the religious institutes are evidence that, involved in the life of the Church, they succeeded in being the Church to the poor and the sick, above all to those most in need of her maternal activity.

How many times Pope Pius XII, and now, Pope Paul VI, repeated to religious women: "You are the heart of the Church. You are the expression of the maternity of the Church."

St. Francis de Sales found a way to make the religious life take a step forward. Unfortunately, he could not actualize it, and had to content himself with an Order of the Visitation which did not match his ideal. The Lord continued this inspiration in St. Vincent de Paul, who was able to transform the world into a convent, launching his Daughters out into all the streets of Paris. Others accomplished the same thing in other places.

Thus, far from being an accusation or criticism, the aggiornamento to which we are called is a simple response to a vital law which has always accompanied the religious life. With a keener awareness of the needs of the Church today, we are continuing to do what has always been done within our institutes following an unchanging characteristic. Not revolution, then, but evolution, is the law of life; it is *dynamic fidelity*.

Such an orientation should also be firmly kept in mind in order to avoid the extreme of immobility, which would signify sickness and death. This immobility would make it easy to say, "Everything has already been done." There is always something to be done further and better. We have no difficulty in admitting that there is something to be changed, transformed, completed and made more efficient in response to contemporary needs and circumstances.

However, let us not put everything and everyone under fire. This should not be done. In a recent article a fine American sister asked: "What is there in our religious life which is weak and sick, which needs to be reinvigorated and cured in order to be more efficient?" Yes, this examination must be made. But let us be careful not to want to change everything.

It is necessary always to remember: "That they may be one," so as not to hold fast to particulars to the detriment of the Church as a whole.

BALANCED CHARACTERIZATION

When we speak of adaptation, this should be understood in a manner consonant with our individual institutes. The principles laid down by the Church are valid and necessary for all, but their application is left to each institute.

This is why the Church has not given many specific directives, nor has she adopted an assembly line system of adaptation, as if taking the whole task upon herself. The Church has laid down the principles of adaptation, but she has also stated that it is up to each institute to adopt these principles and adapt them to itself.

Of course, we should look at other institutes also, since we are not an island in the midst of the Church, yet every institute has its own position and its own special character, and this specific nature of religious institutes must be defended and sustained.

Adaptation should reflect a content, follow a method and be gradual. The norms are to be accepted in a spirit of faith, received with docility and translated into life, but in a manner responsive, harmonious and suited to the individual institute.

We must receive these norms with equilibrium; we must receive them with standards. What the others are doing does not necessarily have to be done by us, too. There should be no isolationism, for we are part of a vital movement from which we must not withdraw ourselves; nonetheless, a medicine which is good for one is not good for all.

Some leaves must fall and some new shoots bud forth. Adaptation expresses renewal, and is grafted on to it in such a life-giving way that we cannot speak of true renewal unless this flows into adaptation.

APOSTOLIC COMPETENCE

True renewal should lead to a spiritual formation more aware, more vital and more complete. It is not enough for religious to be souls of prayer. Whenever they are truly such, they have the duty of being better prepared in religious culture, in their profession, in the care of the sick, in teaching...not only with social graces, but also with that professional competence requisite in our times. In this, religious ought to excel, since theirs is a ministry. Theirs is an apostolate, and not merely a means to financial gain or sustenance.

The commitment in formation is both to the religious life and to the apostolate. The commitment to keep oursevles up to date is an expression of love and of a felt, vital and authentic religious life.

That particular manner of governing which solidly unites the members of the community and makes them collaborators in the promotion of aggiornamento, is religious life and an expression of love of God.

Group discussion is one of the most up-to-date resources of sound pedagogy. It is to be highly esteemed as an expression of community life and as the best experience of religious aggiornamento.

ORGANIC STRUCTURING

Now let us move on to treat the *subject and criteria of adaptation*.

The subject is sketched in broad strokes in *Perfectae Caritatis*, n. 3:

> "The manner of living, praying and working should be suitably adapted everywhere, but especially in mission territories, to the modern physical and psychological circumstances of the members and also, as required by the nature of each institute, to the necessities of the apostolate, the demands of culture, and social and economic circumstances."

Manner of living is a translation of the Latin expression *"ratio vivendi,"* which more than manner means: *structure, system, organization.*

The second paragraph of the same article speaks of the "manner of governing"—*ratio regiminis*—but this does not mean the manner of governing so much as the structure, organization and system of governing.

Ratio refers to something much more complex than what we translate into English as *manner*.

The *ratio vivendi* embraces the very plan of the life of the community. The *ratio orandi* (manner of praying) indicates the content and expression of our prayer, its dispositions, time and place in our schedule and the possibility of a time for individual, personal prayer in addition to community prayer. The *ratio operandi* (manner of working) refers to the type of activity, the methods of working and the systems which we adopt in carrying out our undertakings.

The decree consecutively treats the *ratio vivendi* of contemplatives, of monks, of religious of active life, of brothers, of secular institutes, and so forth.

It should be noted well that we are speaking here of *suitable adaptation*—adaptation appropriate for the institute.

Each of the three spheres of activity (living, praying and working) is basically delineated in other articles of *Perfectae Caritatis* and in other conciliar documents.

The apostolate, for example, is spoken of in *Perfectae Caritatis*, n. 20, and in *Christus Dominus*, nn. 33 and 35, which repeat that we must adapt to the needs of the Church in accord with the necessities of time and place, setting in motion the most appropriate means in the pastoral field.

The system of governing is treated in *Perfectae Caritatis*, n. 14, which takes up obedience and sets forth for superiors and subjects the manner of practicing obedience and exercising authority, so that the two realities—obedience and command—may together be grounded in the exercise of the will of God, in a unique reality which is communion with the Lord.

This does not refer solely to hierarchical structure, but also to the spirit which should animate it. Aggiornamento is much deeper and adaptation deals with an interior spirit.

CONSECRATION OF THE WORLD

What are the *criteria?* The text lists a variety of them: some concern the particular circumstances of the individual religious; others are to be inferred from the environment of time and place in which one labors or from the type of activity which the religious are called upon to perform. Thus, there are *criteria on the basis of the religious, on the basis of the environment* and *on the basis of the type of apostolate.*

This again reminds us that the Church and the religious life must become incarnate in the world of today. The Church enters into human history in every time and every place.

These criteria are valuable everywhere, and carry particular weight with regard to mission lands. Adaptation is not a matter of details and particulars; rather it is an expression of the law which rules the life of the Church and the religious life, according to which the Church must enter into history and absorb human life in its concreteness.

It is thought that only the laity are to sanctify and consecrate the world. Yes, in their sector; but the religious too, must consecrate the world. The religious life is the clearest and most fruitful expression of the world's consecration. We offer ourselves to the religious profession not only as individuals, but as expressions of humanity; we are chosen by the Lord to be religious not only in a personal status, but in a social status—or, indeed, in the name of mankind. *I am the Lord,* He declares. In choosing those of His subjects to whom He gives the call, God wishes to express His rights as king, sovereign and Lord with relation to humanity, and the choice personifies the call of all mankind, incarnate in the religious.

The incarnation of the Word of God is the source of the liberation and redemption of humanity, which by the man, Adam, had fallen, and was redeemed in another man, Jesus Christ.

By analogy, the same thing came about in Mary at the moment of the annunciation. St. Bernard describes the Blessed Virgin to us as the humble Virgin of Nazareth, but also as the representative of humanity, united to God's redemptive plan. In the incarnation of the Word, Mary accepted the redemption in the name of mankind.

The mystery of Mary's divine maternity closely touches all humanity. Our religious vocation, too, is a vocation of all humanity.

Thus, we can better understand how awareness and fidelity in the living of the religious vocation should take into consideration contemporary humanity, with its current needs and present circumstances. These are the *sign* of God, and should be taken into account, so that all may be consecrated to Him.

We present ourselves at the altar with our own humanity and that of others, so that this entire world of ours, with its weaknesses, may be consecrated to God and accepted by Him. With religious profession we consecrate the whole world to God.

From this viewpoint, adaptation signifies consecration.

The training of the religious for the profession of nurse, teacher, social worker, and so forth, is part of the religious life itself. The profession of nurse, teacher, and so forth, is attained through the religious. Thus is the profession transformed into apostolate.

It is up to the individual religious to consecrate his work of nurse or teacher in a particular way, and almost to sum up in himself all the work that each profession involves and offer it all to the Lord as a holocaust.

This is the canticle of the creatures, of the Poverello of Assisi.

Adaptation, therefore, makes us faithful to our religious life and is the consecration of the world, of humanity and of profession. It is the acceptance and consecration of technology, of learning—of all—in the name of the Church.

May the Mother of God help us view in this light that adaptation which will make us ever better and ever more perfectly religious—that is, consecrated to God—in our person which He has called by a special vocation out of all of humanity with its needs, exigencies and present necessities.

CHAPTER 17

PRINCIPLES FOR ADAPTATION

We should dwell on the theme of adaptation, and therefore on the principles which shape it. We have already said that adaptation is the continuation of renewal. It coincides with what is called the *consecration of the world,* especially for those religious institutes dedicated to apostolic activity and receiving the influence of the world as an enrichment, a determination, a concretization of the religious life, which is necessarily in a state of development.

On the one hand, this exact concept of adaptation will prepare us even spiritually for the task of adaptation, so that the proposals considered will never mitigate or lessen the religious life; on the other hand, this concept will prevent us, in our proposals and decisions, from overlooking anything contrary to the religious life and favorable to its mitigation.

GENUINE UPDATING

The spiritual outlook with which to prepare for and decide upon adaptation, should be the result of a renewal sought and seen in contact with the genuine sources of the religious life. These sources are like the filter or seive through which adaptation must pass in order to be authentic. Such a spiritual outlook should aid us and prepare us to accept whatever competent authority will decide and resolve upon under the inspiration of the Holy Spirit and the guidance of the Church.

This criterion of principles of adaptation is the same as that of principles of renewal; it must be followed exactly, to assure to our religious life the primacy of the spiritual life, understood as soul, as motive principle of all our activity.

These principles must guarantee our encounter with God; but spiritual life in itself is not the only encounter with God, since there is also the encounter with God in one's neighbor, in the apostolate, in the duties of human relations and social service. Unity is necessary in our life. We must pull down every wall of separation.

Our spiritual life is of great importance, and must animate our whole being and all our activity. It is not only the vivifier of our intimate contact with God in Holy Communion and in prayer, but it is also the soul of our relationships with our superiors, our fellow religious and all our neighbors. Everything within us should be spiritual life, even if this spiritual life must be concretized in something tangible.

The spiritual life also permeates our body, moves our organism and expresses itself in all our actions.

The Person of the Word united all of human nature to Himself, and permeated all of Christ's humanity with Himself, so that each of His gestures, each of His words, each of His deeds, is divine.

The religious life must be lived in the present moment—in the today of the Church. We shall always have to adapt to the circumstances of the hour. The norms we are examining are not norms of the moment; they are permanent norms, since the Council has not intended to make a concrete plan, a five-year-plan, as it were; these norms are something which permeate all of life and remain.

The demands of the times can also change, but the principles of adaptation do not; the concept is always the same, because it is a law of life, which can neither be transgressed nor attacked.

The principle has an immutable worth and never impairs the eternal values of the religious life. Let this be very clear and distinct in our mind.

SUITABLE UPDATING

We refer to the criteria followed for adaptation or updating as wellsprings and norms. Therefore, what are the criteria, principles or fonts according to which adaptation is to be accomplished?

They are expressed in *Perfectae Caritatis*, n. 3: "The manner of living, praying and working should be *suitably* adapted everywhere...."

What is this suitability? It is this: the style or method by which updating becomes an expression of religious life. That "congruenter," translated with the English word *suitably*, does not mean suitable in measure or quantity but suitable in *quality*.

There are two general criteria expressed in the decree. Let us now examine the first, which is *adaptation to the modern physical and psychological circumstances of religious.*

ADAPTATION TO PHYSICAL POWERS

The manner of living and working should take into account the physical powers of today's religious. Physical health is not very robust today. In organizing the religious life, therefore, the quantity of these energies, and the necessities and needs of spending them in the exercise of the apostolate, must be kept in mind.

Our religious life should value energies for the ministry, for ecclesial service. Long prayer vigils, sleeping on a hard floor or fasting extensively would be absurd, for our spiritual life is a life which translates itself into service, and service requires commitment and physical resistence. This does not mean pampering brother donkey, but it does mean having a supernatural outlook even in regard to the body, for it was given us not so we would annihilate it, but so it would serve us according to the good purposes willed by the Lord.

Missionaries are told: "Do not exhaust your health in a week or a year." The same should be said in terms of adaptation. The lawgivers of the religious life certainly would not be inclined to give in on this point.

The religious life can no longer be organized as it was at one time, with many penances, vigils and strict fasts. This does not mean that there is no place for mortification. Ours is not a Church of mortification as an end in itself. Mortification is ordered to life. The mortification demanded by study and by bedside vigils is in the very nature of life. The positive aspect of mortification takes into account the exigencies inherent in the form of religious life consecrated to works of apostolate.

ADAPTATION TO PSYCHOLOGICAL FACTORS

The principle states further that we must adapt to psychological circumstances. It is necessary to pay much heed to this, for within each of us there is a psychophysical complex which can neither be ignored nor neglected in its evolution and expressions. Such psychical and psychological expressions may be subject to ebb and flow; one thinks of nuances of character, of tendencies, of the various temperaments, of the passions viewed psychosomatically.

There is a psychical education which should be given and which exerts a wide influence. For example, in regard to emotions, there is behavior which should be taken into account and which has aspects varying from place to place. We have to take ourselves as we are.

In the conciliar documents it is stated that the Church does not identify herself with any culture, with any particular expression, even though she was concretized in a Latin world.

Those who take care of formation well know that the temperaments of today's youth are not those of some years ago, and that the temperament of one individual is not that of another. The same may be said of attitudes. We must keep such diversity in mind, in order suitably to foster the formation, education and maturation of religious. Even the manner of educating to chastity, for example, has undergone a change in keeping with the times. There is a psychical affective maturity which must be given, and which is the safeguard of chastity itself. Although with the vows we have renounced positive values, beautiful things, goods which are surely highly esteemed—emphasizes *Lumen Gentium*, n. 46—the vows become a way of completing and marvelously integrating the human personality.

In regard to chastity there is a psychical affective maturity to which one must be educated and which should be lived as the integration of the entire human person. Not all temperaments are capable of chastity. There are some persons who would be unable to bear the religious life because certain of their psychological aspects are not in conformity with it; such persons are certainly not suitable for the religious life. There is a vocation to perfect chastity which is not for all. Perhaps something has influenced the youth of today. We cannot suppress the reality of this psychological evolution; we must only keep it in mind.

In the area of obedience, too, other factors have to be weighed. Obedience is and remains a full, total submission. The Ignatian expression "like a corpse" is widely criticized, and some would like to suppress it. But it remains, in the sense of one who is doubly alive, since he has made the decisions of others his own. We must form religious to the sense of these paradoxes, which are to be found throughout Sacred Scripture, and which we must understand in their full significance: "He who seeks his own life will lose it and he who loses it will gain it" (Jn. 12:25); "If anyone wishes to come after me, let him deny himself..." and then "...take up his cross and follow me" (Mt. 18:24). These are words of eternal life.

In the practice of obedience we should keep in mind the data of contemporary psychology. Today obedience should be presented as a free choice, an enrichment of personality. Today many religious wish to understand the reason behind what is commanded. An order given tactfully and accompanied by some explanation leaves obedience valid; however, this does not give the religious the right to know all the reasons. Otherwise, there would be no more obedience, and the religious would end up obeying himself.

It should be remembered that the time for subduing for the sake of subduing or contradicting for the sake of contradicting, is now past.

Let life in community have a family atmosphere, where everything is presented as a communion of service.

Perhaps this doctrine has been to some extent forgotten. Adaptation of the constitutions should indicate a return to the sources, to the primitive rules. There are human elements which should be resumed to the letter, because they are necessary.

Thus, there is something to consider in the family problem. At one time relatives were more accustomed to detachment, and perhaps there was not as much need to perform an apostolate among them as there is today. Our dealings with relatives could perhaps undergo some adaptation in accord with modern psychological practice. The affective circumstances of today may require more frequent encounters and perhaps even some return into the midst of the family, always with an apostolic attitude, never to water down the religious life.

This holds true, too, for conversations with relatives in the parlor. These days, another's presence at the conversation provokes some feeling of repugnance. The air of espionage makes for closed hearts.

So, too, there is a certain feeling about the supervision of correspondence. This is not to say that the right to supervise letters should be suppressed. However, such a right must be exercised with great delicacy, and it is not stated that the superior necessarily has to read the letters. Much prudence is necessary in the exercise of this right!

Perhaps some alteration in this regard might be introduced into the future Code of Canon Law. Moreover, the Code is not explicit in requiring the supervision of correspondence; such a right is deduced from the fact that the Code specifies what correspondence is to be exempt from supervision. Much care must be given this, and let us say at once that it is not for the individual superiors to make themselves judges of adaptation in this regard. One must adhere to one's own constitutions until the adaptations sanctioned by competent authority intervene.

Relaxation, recreation and vacations should also be considered with psychological sense. It is very useful that the period of refectory reading be brief, since in some cases meals are the only times when members of a community can see one another and talk together.

There is a great need for fraternal gatherings and relaxation. The more a religious feels himself at ease and loved in his community, so much the less will he feel the need of begging comfort and affection elsewhere.

Perfectae Caritatis, n. 15, points out the family spirit and atmosphere of brotherly love within a community as a very effective means to the safeguarding of chastity.

UPDATING IN ACCORD WITH
SOCIAL EXIGENCIES

Then there follows the second criterion of adaptation, *the necessities of the apostolate:* demands of culture and of social and economic circumstances which must be kept in mind.

In the revision of the constitutions it is well to retain the existing valid elements, adding new ones; however, this is never to be a pretense of making a treatise in which everything has to be said, and at length. Things have to be said in a concise but effective manner, leaving it up to the intelligence and heart of the reader to understand the meaning therein, and leaving him free to search out what has already been indicated, but which will be found at greater length in the directory and doctrine of the individual institute. The constitutions should contain permanent and stable principles, which will hold true forever and illumine the contemporary situation.

So that the fruits of the Council may attain their full development *as soon as possible,* it is necessary that religious institutes promote a new spirit within themselves before all else. Hence, the motu proprio *Ecclesiae Sanctae.*

Where shall we begin? With each of us, through our interior attitude, through our spiritual life.

CHAPTER 18

ADAPTATION TO APOSTOLIC NECESSITIES

Let us continue to meditate upon the criteria of adaptation. These criteria demand work on our part—work which is right at hand and, above all, interior.

The work of adaptation also requires action, correspondence and actualization on the part of individuals.

When the persons involved have responsibility, this singular obligation increases. It then involves examination, study and resolutions in regard to that particular sphere of responsibility and work.

A position of authority increases responsibility in adaptation, and is required in the task of prompt implementation in its own sphere of action—without, however, making decisions which are within the province of other governing bodies. In fact, not all adaptation appertains to higher governing bodies. Local superiors, too, have their spheres of competence which concern an updating both of their conduct and of the responsibilities of individuals.

Our meditations should prepare us for a personal effort, which should be undertaken in the proper area at once.

PASTORAL PERSPECTIVE

Therefore, the necessities of the apostolate constitute the second criterion of adaptation: a pastoral, apostolic perspective of the religious life.

Perhaps this is the first time that a council has ever given prominence to the apostolic position of the religious;

perhaps it is the first time that a council contemplated the spectacle of this peaceful army of more than a million religious committed to apostolic endeavor in so many and such varied ministries.

In the Council of Trent there was no question of the apostolic aspect of the religious life insofar as this had developed within the environment of the monastery; the phenomenon of the religious apostolic life, in the proportions in which it exists today, did not then exist in the Church.

It is no wonder that in the conciliar labors of Vatican II we note this apostolic outlook, and, consequently, this apostolic preoccupation concerning religious and this need for their adaptation to the demands of the apostolate.

Numbers 8, 9, 10, 18 and 20 of *Perfectae Caritatis* recall us to such necessities of updating the religious life to the demands of the apostolate. This is a logical consequence of the fact that the apostolate is neither undertaken because of determined circumstances, nor is it an emergency and supplementary undertaking; rather, it is a substantial part of the religious life, while the traditional monastic setting is arranged for a specific type of religious life. For a long time the religious life, especially the feminine religious life, was seen and placed in the monastic setting, which in reality is somewhat restricted.

It is a fact that the exigencies of today's apostolate no longer permit the religious life to be lived within the monastic context.

The context, or setting, functions as a means; the apostolate is substance. If difficulties in orientating the apostolate are encountered, and if something has to go, it must be what is accidental.

It is also necessary to avoid the contrary excess: that of considering the religious life as a means for the apostolate, as if the apostolate should be placed on the ground floor and the religious life on the second. This danger is not hypothetical. How many ask: "Are we first religious, or are we first apostles?" Clearly the problem is not expressed well. The apostolate and its demands must be kept in mind and fulfilled; the frame of the picture of the religious life must be adapted to these necessities.

Aggiornamento will cause us to study the most suitable means for fulfilling our apostolic commitment. It will make us change what is no longer fitting or opportune; it will make us introduce new means and practices; it will cause us to turn to new resources.

Adaptation may require us to abandon certain less timely activities and undertake others, always of the same type or in the same sphere of apostolate.

Numbers 22 and 40 of the implementing norms in *Ecclesiae Sanctae,* make most useful suggestions in this regard. Nonetheless, adaptation in the field of apostolate does not concern only the type of undertaking, but the very way of carrying it out, keeping in mind the environment, the concrete circumstances and the proper way of exercising certain ministries. The fields of apostolate are to be reviewed precisely in regard to the manner of performing the apostolate itself. It is not necessary to wait for a chapter in order to do this.

Even at the local level, superiors will give very concrete and particular apostolic directives. Discussions can and should be held on how we must proceed, on what we have the possibility of doing so that our ministry may radiate the most widely and effectively — so that our school will truly function and our ministry will be more up to date. This dialogue should bring out many things which are to be better implemented.

CULTURAL PERSPECTIVE

The second principle of adaptation is inferred from the exigencies of culture, which have a very close tie with the apostolate and, in fact, extend beyond the apostolate.

By culture in the literary or scientific sense, we usually mean the doctrinal, professional and human preparation of the individual, at least to the minimum necessary for the proper execution of one's assignment in his specific apostolic sphere.

But the term *culture* has a much broader significance. It also refers to mentality, the manner of grasping life, the

philosophy of a people among whom one lives, a popula-
tion's character and way of viewing and solving problems.
The Latin culture is not the African, and the African is not
the Asian. The environment of the city is not that of the
country; that of the plains, not that of the mountains. Our
work must be a work in the concrete, and it is necessary to
keep in mind the diversity of territories where it is undertaken. Thus, the labor undertaken in Italy is not the same
that can be carried out in France, or in Spain or in the
Netherlands, nor that which can be undertaken in Switz-
erland or in America.

These are all different environments, with their own
necessities and degrees of culture, which have to be taken
into consideration.

The culture of a young religious of today cannot be
identical with that of someone who has been a religious
for twenty, thirty or forty years. Even within the community
there can be diverse cultures and mentalities, and our manner of living, praying and acting should always take into
consideration the cultures of all. The organizational plans
for certain general chapters asked that the delegates be
chosen from groups of varying ages, so that all cultures
would be represented. No one has a monopoly of knowledge.

The young have much to receive, but also much to give.
In certain communities there can be some young members
who look upon the older ones with an air of superiority, and
older members who regard the young with an air of paternalism. A harmonious effort is necessary, and all should
bridge the gap. Communication and progress will result,
and we shall have the greatest guarantee of continuity.

Such a broad view of culture requires our endeavors
and enriches them, because it thus causes religious to complete one another. Our religious life is signed with this
beautiful seal of completion, through which one enriches
another. Community life finds a better expression of personal enrichment precisely in integration, through the law
of reception and transmission. Everyone has something to
receive and to give.

SOCIAL PERSPECTIVE

There are also exigencies, *social circumstances*, which we ought to bear in mind, since they are linked up with culture and psychology and perhaps more easily offer occasions of difficulties and problems—it not always being easy to distinguish between those genuine social exigencies which manifest the finger of God and those circumstances which represent the wisdom of the world, as St. Paul expressed it.

Sometimes this situation makes us anxious. What can or can't we accept from the social environment? The problem cannot be resolved in an exclusive manner. It is necessary to consider contemporary criteria.

The religious nurse, for example, today has a sphere of action much more vast than that which he or she had many years ago. It must be kept firmly in mind that the religious has to give his own witness, by which not everything socially licit and considered suitable for the world is such for him. We must always safeguard whatever witnesses to the religious life. The world has to understand that there are souls who have chosen a type of life very different from its own. Thoughtful people have no difficulty in recognizing this heroism.

Nevertheless, there are some things required by social exigencies which we must not overlook; as there are, on the other hand, some limits to be drawn.

Social circumstances also lead to the updating of Canon Law, which will entrust new activities to the apostolic endeavor of the woman, since today she is socially capable of involvement in every area.

ECONOMIC PERSPECTIVE

Moreover, there are economic circumstances. These touch upon poverty, the practice of which has to take into account the circumstances of place. A machine which is quite ordinary in America is a luxury in Italy, and would not be according to religious poverty in that nation.

The criteria are not absolutely mathematical; they should be adapted to the various institutes. The proper application of criteria to the demands of adaptation should

bear in mind many circumstances of the individual institute, its own special character, the place where it has to
carry out its apostolate and the type of apostolate carried on.

It is logical that the adaptation undertaken in a cloistered monastery will not be the same as that made in a community where sisters must function as doctors, nurses,
teachers, and so forth.

Adaptation cannot be the same, because the types of
life are diverse, varying from institute to institute. For example, the Daughters of Charity of St. Vincent de Paul have
a type of life quite different from that of the Sisters of the
Assumption.

Moreover, these principles should be applied simultaneously, so that one helps to put the other into effect.
There are many shades of difference. Not for vain and
specious pretexts do we choose this and set that aside; but
only truly to increase our spiritual and apostolic vitality.

Adaptation is also to be effected in the manner of governing, in the system of government, in the manner of deal-
ing with one's own religious. To be considered, of course,
are the psychological element and the more emphatic
communitarian character—that is, the more strongly emphasized communion of mind, heart and soul. Community
is family, just as the primitive Church was one heart and
one soul. It is precisely this concept of community which
should dictate the manner of governing, of guiding, of
ruling. This is not a surrender to the community of the
right to govern. The superior remains the superior. Only
the manner of expressing his mandate changes, since he
is in a community,of sons, of brothers. Let us think of the
community in the Cenacle, where all were united about
Mary. The superior must preside over the community as
Mary did and with her spirit: "Behold the handmaid of the
Lord." Called to play such an important role in the plan of
redemption, Mary presented herself as "handmaid!"

This is the spirit of authority. To be excluded, therefore, is excessive paternalism, by which religious are
treated as perennial children.

The religious life is a mature life, an adult life.

All the foregoing can be accomplished. Indeed, let us do it at once, without waiting for a chapter. In spirit, let us prepare for this adaptation, making all our personal applications, so as to contribute, each in his own capacity, to the true rejuvenation of ourselves and our institute, according to the spirit and will of the Council, thus also contributing to what will be the undertaking of higher authority.

CHAPTER 19

THE RELIGIOUS LIFE IS
THE LIFE OF THE CHURCH

We have steeped ourselves in the mystery of the religious life in order to renew ourselves in it. We have sought to return to the wellsprings of this same life which originated in the following of Christ as presented to us with the special charism granted to our institute. Moreover, we have endeavored to understand better how our institute, with its own special character, may realize such following of Christ in the Church. And this we have done generously, with a desire and zeal for the spread of the kingdom of Christ—always, however, keeping ourselves rooted in Christ, convinced that the spiritual life, union with Him, holds first place.

We have tried to see how this mystery of the religious life should incarnate itself in the contemporary world, and should develop itself according to the divine plan— that is, according to what God has conceived, foreseen and designed for that determined environment, with those particular persons, with those precise requirements.

Under the impulse of the Holy Spirit and with the help of the Mother of God, we now continue our meditation, and view the religious life as configuration to Christ and to Mary, His Mother.

In this meditation, we return to various aspects of this mystery, so as to see how this ideal can be translated into life. We may view the religious life as a participation in the mystery of the cross of Christ. We may view it in the exercise of the theological and moral virtues — in the exercise of charity towards God and neighbor — expressed in the vows, leading to full maturity — to the full measure of the age of Christ — and unfolding as a life of prayer, virtue, devotion, love, community and human relations. Let us look at all this, the better to verify whether or not our practical life is in accord with the concrete, not abstract, *ideal*, who is Jesus Christ. But it will be an individual endeavor, which each can undertake in the silence of his own meditation.

HARMONIZING COMPONENT

We penetrate a little further into the ecclesial component of the religious life. The ecclesial aspect is like the substance of our entire religious life, because to live the Church is to live Christ. Living the Church is the unifying principle of our entire life. *The entire theme of our life has its source in Jesus, as He presents Himself in the Church,* and is ordered toward Jesus in the Church. It is in the Church that our communion with Christ is brought about. Our program is the life of Jesus in the Church, and the life of the Church as a response to Jesus.

The "Decree on Priestly Training" sets forth the concept of the unity and harmony of all life, coordinated and fashioned in Jesus Christ.

Unfortunately, our weakness brings about a certain division, a certain dispersion, a kind of partitioning off which leads to lukewarmness and mediocrity. All this is diametrically opposed to the religious life, which is a unified life, indivision *par excellence,* allowing of no divisions. While weakness brings about dispersion of forces and divisions, we come upon a source of motion, power and strength when we discover a unifying factor. This unifying and vitalizing focal point is undoubtedly the Church. Such unification is actualized in living our life as the life of Christ in the Church, and as the life of the Church in Christ.

The religious life lived under the impulse of the Holy Spirit infuses harmony and unity into our hearts; it brings us always to live nearer to Christ, both for Him and for His Mystical Body, which is the Church.

ESSENTIAL ELEMENT

In *Lumen Gentium,* n. 44, we read:

"Christ proposed to His disciples this form of life, which He, as the Son of God, accepted in entering this world to do the will of the Father. This same state of life is accurately exemplified and perpetually made present in the Church."

Let us note "is made present," that is, *made newly present,* continuing the presence of Jesus. The religious life does not only symbolize and recall the life of Jesus, but it faithfully continues the life of Jesus in the Church.

Accurately.... Every Christian life is an imitation of Christ, but the religious life is a continuation of the life of Christ in a more complete, more intimate and more profound manner.

This luminous reality can give unity, strength and enthusiasm for the living of our religious life in greater depth and interiority; it can make us feel that we are far from insignificant: "Recognize your dignity and live in a manner consistent with what you are in Christ and in the Church!"

The mystery of Christ is a source of unity and strength for our religious life. The Church, mystery of Christ, must live the life hidden with Christ in God, as such. We must live this hidden life in the Church.

The Church is the mysterious environment in which our life unfolds, nourishes itself and perfects itself.

To our ecclesial life we must apply what the priest says in the canon: "through him, with him, in him." By means of You, with You and in You, I want to fashion my life into a hymn of continual praise, an exaltation of You, O Lord, through the Church, with the Church and in the Church.

This formula gives structure to our life; it is the program of the life which we must live for the Church, with the Church and in the Church. We must see and encounter Jesus in the Church, and it is in the Church that we will place ourselves in communion with Him.

May our life unfold *in the Church.* The life of chastity, poverty and of obedience is the life of the Church.

The conciliar documents present the religious life as a *special gift in the life of the Church:* a divine gift which the Church has received from her Lord; as life in the Church, as a sharing in the life of the Church, as a form of life in the Church.

Our entire life should be viewed, lived and programmed in the Church, wherein the mystery of the religious life is such a necessary and substantial element that we cannot imagine the Church without the religious life, understood as a state of consecration, as a particular way of life which has its foundation and *basis* in the profession of the evangelical counsels and its dimensions in poverty, chastity and obedience.

Lumen Gentium, n. 43, declares that the religious state is open to both clerics and laity, to those faithful who "are called by God from both these states of life so that they may enjoy this particular gift in the life of the Church and thus each in one's own way, may be of some advantage to the salvific mission of the Church."

It is, therefore, *a divine gift, a special gift, bestowed by the Lord, upon the life of the Church.*

The last sentence of n. 44 declares that the state constituted by the profession of the evangelical counsels undeniably belongs to the life of the Church and to its holiness; it is not an element of the hierarchical structure or order of the Church; — no one ever thought of such a thing — but it is nonetheless a part of the Church's life and holiness which can never be shaken. It is a part of the Church as a necessary element, so indispensable to her that one cannot conceive of the Church without this state, and this state will always exist within the Church. How many times the Pope has exlcaimed: "The Church needs you."

The last paragraph of *Perfectae Caritatis,* n. 1, recalls the *necessary function* of religious in the Church.

It is a necessary function, because Jesus, who has given Himself to the Church, wants to remain in the Church in the most perfect possible way; He wants His life to endure in the Church as master, sanctifier and sacrificer, as shepherd, but also as *the religious of the Father.*

Jesus wills to prolong this latter attribute and function in the Church. In the priestly ministry He continues His life as master, sanctifier and sacrificer; but priests are not necessarily religious. Holy Orders does not sum up all the aspects of the life of Jesus. As the religious of the Father, Jesus lives in the religious state.

This doctrinal, theological foundation is not only a reality which enlightens; it is also a strengthening and energizing reality which calls for commitment and responsibility on our part.

COMPLEMENTARY REALITY

The necessary function of the religious life also stems from the fact that the Church, spouse of Christ, must correspond to the love of Jesus, her Spouse, in the most complete manner possible.

And the spouse of Christ must represent Christ in herself, make herself similar to Him and give Him souls consecrated in poverty, chastity and obedience.

Were we not generous souls, taking the Church's personality within ourselves as poor and obedient virgins, the Church would not be complete and could not give her Spouse the full testimony of her love.

Through religious souls, the Church presents herself to her Spouse crowned with virginity. The splendor of the virginity of Christ is much more fully reflected in the soul consecrated to Him than it is in the lay person, who comes to Him with a heart shared with another creature, in communion with another creature. Who better than a soul who is consecrated to perfect charity and who gives himself or herself to Christ with an undivided heart — who better than such a soul can continue the virginity of the Son of God in the Church?

And no layman should feel hurt because of this!

While the priest communicates Jesus Master, Jesus Shepherd, Jesus Sanctifier, and renders Him present, the religious makes Jesus present in the Church as the Religious of the Father in a *fuller* manner, that is, in His chastity, in His poverty, in His obedience.

The Lord has given His Church a state of life in which there is a more faithful similarity to Jesus, and this by His mysterious design!

What counts is not the name of religious but the *reality*. If we do not live our religious life well, if we are religious only in name and not in fact, in a certain way we deprive the Church of that holiness which is necessary to her, and in a certain manner we deprive Jesus of the complete gift which He wills to make to His Church. What an obligation and responsibility!

The religious life holds a position in the Church which is completely its own and which is located in the heart of the Church, in holiness.

By a mandate, the institutes consecrated to the apostolate act in the name of the Church. We are the Church, not only in the apostolate, *but especially in the sphere of sanctity*. The Church expresses her holiness through us in a very special way.

Let us ask of the Holy Spirit and the Blessed Virgin that we may come to understand our place and our *raison d'être*, in the Church, so as to live our ecclesial vocation to the full.

CHAPTER 20

THE RELIGIOUS LIFE IS WHOLLY
FOR THE CHURCH

Let us seek to condense the various thoughts expressed in the ecclesial perspective of the religious life into some enduring principle which will help us to live for Jesus, with Jesus and in Jesus within the Church.

Indeed, the Council has brought the Church to encounter herself in Christ and to express Him in herself; thus, it has brought us to encounter ourselves with Christ in the Church and to express Him in the Church.

During the Council when it was discussed whether or not *Lumen Gentium* should contain a special chapter on religious, this was no mere question of procedure; it was instead, a question which would have had substantial repercussions.

If a "Constitution on the Church" had emerged from the Council, articulate in all its elements and lacking a chapter on religious, we would have asked ourselves: "Why? Is there no place for religious in the Church?" Or rather: "Have religious no special classification? Are they unnecessary, then?"

A SEPARATE CHAPTER

So great was its importance that the question of procedure was brought before the full conciliar assembly, and it was neither the central commission nor the mixed commission which treated it, but the general plenary assembly, which decided that there must be a special chapter entitled *De Religiosis.*

Chapter 6 of *Lumen Gentium* was elaborated in the mixed commission, that is, in the combined commissions for the Faith and for religious.

All were unanimous in emphasizing the religious life in the bosom of the Church. There was more of an inclination to place it in chapter 5, which treats of the universal call to sanctity. It was said that the fitting place for the religious was there, within the context of the Church's holiness.

If a special chapter had not been devoted to the religious life, many problems would have arisen. And what disastrous results there would have been, including the repercussion on vocations. What would today's youth ever have thought?

We thank the Lord for letting Himself be won by many prayers and we treasure His marvelous gift of Chapter 6.

There was also an analogous question regarding the Blessed Mother. Should a special decree be issued on Mary, or should a chapter be added as an insert in the constitution *Lumen Gentium?*

The Lord knows how to write straight even with crooked lines. In order to prevent the treatise on the Mother of God from being reduced to a minimum, there were some who insisted that Mary be treated separately, in a special document. But the Holy Spirit was at work. And now we have the *mother present in the Church.* Let us thank the Lord.

What idea of the Church should we have had, if there had not been a chapter on the Blessed Mother?

RAISON D'ÊTRE

The chapter on religious places the religious in the Church as a part thereof—a necessary part, inasmuch as the Church has a longing to conform herself to her celestial Spouse, and inasmuch as she must reproduce in herself the form of life which Jesus Himself lived. And how could that be brought about unless there were souls vowed to chastity, poverty and obedience?

The religious life presents itself as a special bond with Christ, which expresses itself in the Church, with the Church, and through the Church.

The Blessed Mother, too, has her chapter in *Lumen Gentium*. She presents herself as a special bond which links her to the Church as mother, and the life of the Blessed Mother is the life of the Church. Thus, Mary is bound to the Church, and is the Church.

Our affirmation that to live with the Church, for the Church and in the Church corresponds to living with Christ, for Christ and in Christ — also holds true for living with Mary, for Mary and in Mary.

The one explains the other. *Lumen Gentium,* n. 65, states:

"While in the most holy Virgin the Church has already reached that perfection whereby she is without spot or wrinkle, the followers of Christ still strive to increase in holiness by conquering sin. And so they turn their eyes to Mary who shines forth to the whole community of the elect as the model of virtues. Piously meditating on her and contemplating her in the light of the Word made man, the Church...becomes more and more like her Spouse."

This continual conforming to Christ, the Church has accomplished in Mary and is accomplishing in religious.

The religious life places us fully within the mystery of Jesus in the Church, and in the mystery of Mary, mother and daughter of the Church.

The religious life is a life which develops for the Church, is finalized by the Church, and has the Church herself as its aim and end.

At the very beginning of the chapter on religious in *Lumen Gentium,* it is beautifully noted that the religious life, founded on the words and examples of the Lord, is a gift which God made to His Church; it has arisen for the good of the Church.

The religious life is a consecration to God which expresses itself in consecration to the Church; it is service to

God, but in the Church. It is ordered to the sanctification of the Church, to the building up of the body of Christ. We are living stones which must one by one construct the Church in depth and in extension. *The Church is the raison d'être of the religious life.*

BOND OF JUSTICE

Therefore, our profession receives content and develops itself in breadth more than we think. In profession it is the Church herself who consecrates herself to God. The riches and treasures are not only for me, but the religious life is ordered to the Church, and is altruistic *par excellence:* it has a social character in the most eminent degree. It is oblational love; a continual seeking of the good of all.

The religious life is not an introverted life; it does not withdraw into itself. It is a life of openness to others in God; in it God encounters humanity, and humanity encounters God.

Our life is really a holocaust in which we place ourselves at the disposition of all; it has no limits of affection, of economic goods, of personal interest; our very liberty is for others. Every personal interest is suppressed and we enter into our innermost being, into our liberty, which we give a social orientation, a direction which brings us out of ourselves to enrich others.

An orientation of this kind gives a sublime sense of our vocation and acts upon us.

"But am I all this?" Yes, I am all this. The more we are religious, the more dynamic is the life of the Church and the more fervent is her apostolate, for the Church lives through us and we live for the Church and of the Church.

This is not a living with the Church only by a bond of affection. With religious profession we bind ourselves with the bond of justice—with the bond of religion, with the bond of love and fidelity. The institute is of the Church, and the Church pervades the entire institute.

RADICAL POSSESSION

We must serve the Church in our institute. Our ecclesial service, *our diaconia*, becomes a commitment, and everything within us must be directed to the Church. In the religious life we give the Church everything. If we can do something, we must do it for the Church. We belong to the Church down to the very roots of our life. Our every service is ecclesial. There is nothing in us which does not belong to the Church.

There is no other category of persons in the bosom of the Church who belong to her as totally as we religious.

The priest has a sphere of action under his private dominion — disposal of time, means, actions and organization, for example. Instead, in the life of the religious there is nothing which can be *his*. The religious life is ecclesial in its totality. Everything in it is of the Church, and it is no wonder that the Church regards this way of life as being always and entirely under her jurisdiction.

Our material goods are ecclesiastical goods; that is, they are goods which belong to the Church. Everything appertaining to the religious is at the disposal of the Church, and the Church can dispose of it as she deems best for her own good, so that, without any injustice, the Pope could ask for a house or piece of land in order to meet ecclesial needs.

PERFECT COMMITMENT

There is an aspiration and ambition, partially lawful, to assert one's own personality. Now, our personality as religious is the Church. If, therefore, we are given an objective or an order which is contrary to our tastes, we must remember that we did not say, when making profession: "I will obey myself." We made the vow to God, through the Church and into the hands of the Church. And the Church has the right to dispose of us. No wonder, then, that she takes us at our word.

"He must increase, but I must decrease" (Jn. 3:30). At the apex of our desires, we must not place the ego, but the Church, and it is for her that we must live.

However, the Church is not a force which swallows us up and depersonalizes us. It is precisely in her, instead, that we find our maturity, the full expression of ourselves, our fulfillment, according to the design and plan of God.

Nothing forced me to become a religious. I became a religious through the Church and in the Church. It is for the Church that I must work, and my service is ecclesial. Therefore, I must feel myself obliged to do my duty well and to lead those entrusted to me, with a true ecclesial sense and fidelity to the Church.

These ideas, *as a principle,* should enter into the constitutions and into the program of formation. The motu proprio *Ecclesiae Sanctae,* n. 12a, expressly recommends that the constitutions express the bond, the union, between the religious life and the Church.

Let us recall what the archangel said to the Virgin: "You will conceive and bring forth a son: he will be the redeemer, the Savior." At that moment the Blessed Virgin was elevated to her high dignity for the benefit of the Church. The Mother of God gave the Church her Son, but she also gave herself, incarnating the motto-program: "to live for the Church." Could not this also be our motto?

CHAPTER 21

OBEDIENCE IS A GUARANTEE
OF ECCLESIAL LIFE

At a certain moment, our prayer life gives us the same impression the disciples had upon climbing the mount of the transfiguration. They had become tired in climbing to the summit. Then, contented and fascinated by the splendid light radiating from Christ, they exclaimed, "It is good for us to be here!" (Mk. 9:4) If life were always thus, we would go ahead happily. The Lord would be content with us and we with Him. But we must descend the mount, and as we descend there is the danger that our fervor will wane. Rather, we must bring this transfiguration with us, *this* aura of light, *this* enthusiasm which the Lord has communicated to us, *this* attitude of joy and of readiness to follow Him wherever He wishes.

Our transfiguration must not be effected in an abstract, theoretical way, but in a concrete manner, just as the Lord has arranged it for us.

With our ecclesial life we live in Christ within the Church. And in the Church, in Christ, we live *for* the Church, because we are at her service, consecrated to her.

"They have dedicated their entire lives to His service. This constitutes a special consecration.... Since the Church has accepted their surrender of self they should realize they are also dedicated to its service" (*Perfectae Caritatis*, n. 5).

Our life must be lived for the Church in whole, globally, and in detail. However, we need to feel something within us that truly integrates us into the Church, keeps us in the Church and makes us live in the Church. We need something that truly assures us of our tie with the Church, makes us live with her and in her, and gives us a guarantee of living in dependence upon her.

And what gives us such a guarantee?

It is obedience — submission. Number 14 of *Perfectae Caritatis,* which treats of obedience, is an article which is rich, binding, and also encouraging.

COMMUNION WITH THE DIVINE WILL

It may come spontaneously to ask: "But how can I realize a continually ecclesial life? How can I be the Church, and how can the Church be in me to permeate my entire life, all my work and each of my tasks?"

The means by which our ecclesial life is realized in an earnest, authentic and infallible way, is obedience — not, however, conceived as we ourselves will or think; understood in this latter sense, obedience could be dependence, not upon the Church but upon our own will, upon ourselves with our criteria and tastes.

Obedience gives us assurance and concretizes our ecclesial life through the offering of ourselves to God, immolating our will and placing us in communion with God's will — His sacrificial will — in a sure manner.

Through the vow of obedience, the religious places himself in a state of immolation of his own will in regard to God — immolation which signifies the acceptance of the will of God and the plunging of one's own will into that of God, thus setting up a contact of the will of the religious with the saving will of God; then the love of God, the very life of God, is placed at the base and center of the religious life.

This is why the vow of obedience enables us to work through the Church. By it, the will of God becomes the driving force of our entire life, as it was for the life of Jesus with regard to His Father.

The vow of obedience binds our will always to do God's will, to incorporate ourselves into the will of God. Thus the will and love of God enter within us and work in us.

However, the vow of obedience is not to be regarded solely as a union of our will with that of God; the whole life of God is communicated to us and works in us, and all our life enters into God.

As a result of obedience the love of God flows into us, inundates us and makes our life become divine.

That is how the vow of obedience should be presented in the constitutions, also. The vow is not only a commitment to do the will of the Lord; it is *a state of communion with God in the Church*, through obedience.

SIGN OF AUTHENTICITY

The Church is a sacrament of union with God and of unity with one's brethren.

With the vow of obedience, made to God in the Church, I am integrated into the Church in a special way and enter into communion of life with God and with my brothers, in the accomplishment of God's will transmitted to me through the Church.

Herein lies our surety. Through the obedience of the Son of God, I am assimilated to the Word, who with the Father and the Holy Spirit comes to me, communicates Himself in obedience in a true and concrete manner, gives me the certainty that everything that I will do in the name of obedience is what God wants of me.

This is the richness of obedience. This is how it acquires a theological, spiritual and apostolic content; this is how it becomes thoroughly dynamic. It makes me share in the richness of Jesus in His union with the Father, in His union with the Church, and in His salvific will and redemptive work. Hence: obedience has not only a juridical content; obedience is not merely a source of a duty or the fulfillment of a duty of dependence. Obedience has a theological, spiritual and apostolic content which is working throughout my entire being with an incredible dynamism; it is working in the dimensions of holiness, of worship and of apostolate.

But all of this requires a concretization. This implies the designation on God's part of someone who assures me, in His name, that I am doing His will.

Number 14 states that religious, under the impulse of the Holy Spirit, submit themselves in a spirit of faith to their superiors, who are the representatives of God.

Between myself and God, as a guarantee of that communion between us, God places authority; He places persons who act in His stead, who are like the sacrament of God, the sign of my union with God.

We should be very grateful to God for His gift of authority.

In the religious life, where contact with God must be fuller, more complete and more intimate, we have persons who constantly and authentically assure us of His will. These are our superiors, who represent God.

No one can take upon himself the right of representing God. But God Himself can have Himself represented in a sure manner.

We have the Lord in the Eucharist, in Sacred Scripture and in authority. Religious authority has a vast sphere of activity, governing our whole life, exactly because of the importance which the religious life has in the Church. There is nothing which is not the province of authority. The life which we place in the hands of God through obedience, is under the safeguard of authority. Even in regard to the service of all our brothers in Christ, authority guides us and assures us that we are coming to their aid in a genuine manner.

IN THE PLAN OF GOD

Through obedience religious "are closely bound to the service of the Church." And it is still obedience which makes us reach the fullness of personality development, because obedience makes us "attain to the measure of the full manhood of Christ."

In a spirit of faith and of love for the will of God, and in line with what the constitutions prescribe, religious must therefore humbly obey their superiors — the decree continues — placing all the forces of their intellect and will and the gifts of nature and grace at the disposition of their superiors, collaborating in the building up of the body of Christ according to the plan of God.

When I am in the plan of God, I know that I am myself. "In this way, religious obedience, far from lessening the dignity of the human person, by extending the freedom of the sons of God, leads it to maturity."

The offering of one's own liberty, as a sacrifice of oneself, brings about a maturation of liberty in the religious. One does not attain maturity by abandoning himself to his own will.

When our will is offered in sacrifice, then we enter upon life with the fullness of development and of liberty.

Our personality is not something which stands up of itself; our personality is whatever God wants of us, integrating us into His plan. We are something, to the extent that we are within the plan of God. We have the maximum of personality when we find ourselves within the divine design.

Man is great only when he communicates with the greatness of God, inserting himself in His plan and keeping himself within it through obedience to God's representatives.

Authority's activity in our religious life is not undue interference. It is God who comes to us; it is His hand that extends itself toward us, to draw us to Him. We must deem ourselves fortunate to be able always to have this hand of God to bind us, guide us, draw us to Himself and transmit His love to us.

Thus, the source of authority in the religious life is not my will or my free choice. It is the Lord Himself who has given authority to my superior, through the Church.

How important has the intervention of Church authority been in the erection of our institutes! It is true that the institutes arise by themselves; however, they become religious institutes in the full sense when they receive the approbation of the Church, which blesses them with something of its own authority.

For example, when the chapter is convened, it is not the capitulars who give authority to the superior general. It is the Church which, through the rules, confers authority upon him. Thus also, the local superiors, named by the superior general, derive their authority from the Church.

Through authority, which comes from the Church, I have the guarantee of finding myself in the heart, will and design of God. Have we not perhaps said that obedience places us in communion with God and with our brethren and inserts us into the complete, total plan of God, through the Church?

THE MORE, THE BETTER

If this reality is a source of joy for religious, it is also a source of duties, not only juridical, but above all theological. If I am placed in vital contact with God, I ought to give the Lord my all—energies of body, mind and heart, energies of grace and of the supernatural gifts I have received. I am not a simple laborer; I am a friend who enters into communion with God, and therefore the norm of my adhesion to God is: "the more, the better."

Obedience should be understood on a level of love and not so much on a level of rights and duties. If I place myself on a juridical level, I begin to make distinctions between rights and duties, with the result that the will can be tempted to be its own authority. The laity and the clergy have kept a sphere of free initiative. In this area they do not have the security of obedience.

The religious, instead, has reserved no sphere of action to himself. In obedience, he has given all, and for love. "The more, the better" is his attitude, because it is a relationship of love, and love does not haggle, weigh or measure.

Our obedience must be given and lived as a gift, as a holocaust; nothing, then, should be spared.

The more we depend on the authority to whom we entrust ourselves, the greater security will we have.

When I entrust myself to the superior, I do not abandon myself automatically, like a machine. The automatic pilot of religious obedience does not exist; religious obedience requires active participation—the total participation of our entire being.

Our obedience is always constructive and creative; that is, it develops our dynamism and engages all our resources and potential in its activity.

Obedience requires that we bring all our own gifts of nature and grace to the task at hand.

It is an act of obedience responsibly to take initiative in one's own sphere of activity, and the superior is to leave the possibility of this to his religious.

AUTHORITY IN A SPIRIT OF SERVICE

If this is the reality of the vow of obedience, side-by-side with submission *there is also authority*. Those who are vested with this service, this ministry of authority, must accomplish it on a theological basis. The decree *Perfectae Caritatis* states:

"Superiors...should fulfill their office in a way responsive to God's will." (That is, in obedience and submission to the major superiors.) "They should exercise their authority out of a spirit of service to the brethren, expressing in this way the love with which God loves their subjects."

Obedience is communion. Authority is given for the building up of the body of Christ; in its turn, it is communion with God and with the brethren, and is an act of charity.

The right of ownership is personal, but authority is not ownership. The religious belong to the Lord, and I must serve them in such a way as to show them the heart of God, the love of God, the hand of God. Rights, which are not absolute, must be framed within the love of God.

Since obedience contributes to the realization of the plan of God, he who guides must do so while permitting those who obey to give themselves totally, bringing them to be ever more children of God. Therefore, he should treat his subjects as children of God, with respect for the human person.

The abuse of authority is almost a sacrilege, for it is an abuse of something sacred. Authority is given to us not for ourselves, but for others.

AUTHORITY, BRIDGE OF UNION

If the exercise of authority should perhaps be re-examined in aggiornamento, authority in itself cannot be: otherwise there would be no more vow of obedience.

If we had to remove the point of contact, everything would come to a standstill. We would not be in communion with God if there were no longer this welding between Him and us.

Authority is necessary to assure us of the love of God. Obedience enables us to work through the Church. Authority is the energy that comes to us from the Church. Nowadays it is customary to emphasize family spirit, but this is to be rightly understood. The superior is not the presiding officer of a type of discussion group — or, as is said today, of a round table — taking the ideas of the majority and adopting them himself in order to persuade others. Even if he does avail himself of the ideas of others, the superior has freedom of decision. He it is who has and must retain the authority, so as to guarantee the will of God. Family spirit does not do away with authority.

The superior is not he who sums up the ideas of all, but he who assures us what the will of God is. It is true that, as we have said, he utilizes the counsel of his brethren, especially of those deputed for this.

This spirit of obedience is not oppression of personality or inhibition of initiatives; rather, it creates that family atmosphere in which each member feels at ease and feels duty-bound to contribute to the good of the community.

Authority has the right to intervene, since it has the duty to keep us — even in spite of ourselves — firm in our contact with God and secure in His loving arms. Should there be some breach, it helps us to re-establish our contact with God and with our brethren.

In reaching our individual religious houses, whether the destination pleases or displeases us, we will find ourselves in communion with God, in His will. Certainly we would not be in the will of God were we to wish to remain on Tabor.

"For them I sanctify myself, that they also may be sanctified" (Jn. 17:19): that is my program, and I return so enriched, so illuminated, so consolidated in the love of God, that with my fellow religious I can put God's saving plan into effect, as He wills, as the Church wills, exactly where the Church, through obedience, has placed me.

CHAPTER 22

FIDELITY TO ONE'S OWN RELIGIOUS AND ECCLESIASTICAL VOCATION

The purpose of this meditation is to examine by means of a synthesis and summary the significance of the principle that contains everything which we have said and must do; in other words, our purpose is to see more clearly the content of: "For me to live is the Church."

The religious life involves an altogether special bond with the Church; it is a life wholly ecclesial.

Obedience has shown us the way in which our life is ecclesial. Guided by the Church, it develops by means of Christ, through His influence, by virtue of His strength, which brings us to live in union with the Father and with the Holy Spirit. The divine life expresses itself in us, insofar as our life, with obedience, is inserted in God and participates in the life of God.

Obedience and authority assure us of contact with God and therefore with His love, in such a way that our life, permeated and guided by obedience, develops by means of Christ in the Church.

PARTICIPATION IN THE MISSION OF THE CHURCH

All this is preparatory to another element, another component of the ecclesial life, of our *living the Church*.

Obedience, which unites us to Christ through the Church, also brings about a communication, a sharing by us in the very mission of the Church.

This is why the last article of *Lumen Gentium,* chapter 6, urges *that we persevere and ever grow in the vocation to which the Son of God has called us for the increased holiness of the Church* (cf. n. 47).

Our vocation is the very vocation of the Church, that is, the vocation to holiness. It is not by chance that the chapter on religious follows that on the universal call to holiness, for the religious life is a particular communication of the Church's vocation to sanctity, and at the same time the religious life is a particular expression of this vocation.

Therefore, to live our vocation is to live the Church's vocation, which is — we repeat — the vocation to holiness. In the ceremony of profession the Church made us her own, so that we may live and express her sanctity in a full and perfect manner within us.

The whole structure of the religious life empowers us to participate in the life and mission of the Church; we must actualize our part in the mission of the Church herself.

Our holiness is not a thin stream that runs beside the great river of the holiness of the Church; rather, it is the holiness of the Church, which in us and by means of us aims at radiating Christ and winning others to Him.

The various formulas: "act in the Church," "act through the Church," and "act with the Church," have their nuances. To act with the Church means to make the Church's vocation our own and to realize it in ourselves.

In the Blessed Mother the Church is sanctified and attains her holiness; therefore, the Church's members must look to Mary as to the prototype and model of the Church's sanctity. If that is required of all, it is required especially of those who have their own mission of holiness in the Church.

COMMUNITY, A SMALL CHURCH

What is the identification card of our citizenship in the Church?

Our specific mission in the Church, our title to citizenship, is the Church's holiness, which is realized in us.

Communion in the holiness of the Church means communion in all the dimensions of ecclesial holiness, and therefore in the Church's theological and liturgical vocation and in her apostolic dimension, which expresses for us her vocation to holiness.

Precisely because she is holy, the Church is apostolic; precisely because she yearns for God, she yearns for her neighbor. Here on earth, holiness must bring us to others. Every religious life, which is necessarily apostolic, participates in the structure of community, of assembly, and has a commitment to express the Church in this structure of hers. The Church is the family of the children of God assembled in the Father, in the Son and in the Holy Spirit. The Church is a congregation; it is the people of God; it is a community.

But what, even in its organization and external expressions, manifests the Church as an assembly in a special way?

The religious community, in its expression of communitarian life, of life in common.

With regard to common life, *Perfectae Caritatis*, n. 15, refers to the example of the primitive Church, where the mystery of the Mystical Body was given a much more coherent external expression: a multitude of believers, but one heart and one soul. Every Christian assembly usually lasts an hour or so. It becomes concrete at this liturgical moment, as a family united in the name of the Lord.

The religious life, with its form of life in common, concretizes the life of the Church in a permanent shape, as the people of God, as a congregation.

In the literature of antiquity, the religious community was called the *micro ecclesia*, that is, the little Church.

The reality of the Church is expressed in all its dimensions, shades and tones in our religious communities.

Ideally, the apostolic Church was organized like the religious life. The Church should function and act as a community; it should be more similar to the heavenly Church, where all are united in praising and enjoying the Trinity.

What on this earth expresses and anticipates the heavenly Church? The religious community, which reproduces and testifies to this eschatological reality of the Church.

Even the juridical organization of the religious life is meaningful. The religious life is a gift of God entrusted to the Church, which has accepted, interpreted and organized it, and has linked its structure to her life.

PROPHETIC AND ESCHATOLOGICAL VOCATION

The religious life is communion in the Church's life; thus, it calls for fidelity to all the dimensions of the ecclesial vocation.

Like the Church, the religious life proclaims a future life (prophetic vocation) and keeps before souls the fact of the world to come (eschatological vocation). The religious life is a sign. Its content signifies what awaits us. The religious life is not understood when measured by natural standards; it is understood when evaluated in the light of eternity. We are in this life as on a pilgrimage, since the Church finds her fulfillment in eternity, that is, in the final communion with Jesus.

The religious life is a proclamation of a future life, of the paschal mystery which heralds the reality awaiting us; the Church must be the prophetic voice of this reality. Therefore, we are the Church in her call to holiness, in her mission and in her various dimensions.

If we thus participate in the life of the Church, we must correspond to the Church's vocation. Our life must be so lived that in it everyone may read Christ and the Church: *the Church in us.*

This *presenting of Christ* is the Church's proper mission. The Church is mother; the Church is witness to Christ; the Church is the herald of Christ; and she is all of this in a special way in religious as her representatives. "The Church presents Christ to believers and non-believers alike in a striking manner daily through them," declares *Lumen Gentium.*

The Church must present Christ in the life of religious in such a way that believers and non-believers will see Him in action, will hear Him, will grasp Him. We are like an ostensorium. We are more than that, for our brethren must see and almost touch Jesus Christ in our life as religious.

THINKING WITH THE CHURCH

This calls for our participation in the mind, heart and will of the Church—the complete realization in us of the life of the Church. Now, this will come about when the Church's sentiments will be our own—when her desires, plans, initiatives, conduct and doctrine will be our desires, our plans, our initiatives, our conduct and doctrine. *Everything that is of the Church must become ours.*

We must love and absorb all the thought of the Church: "Think with the Church," that is, savor and share in the sentiments of the Church. This is what the Pope insistently asks of us. The mind, preoccupations and longings of the Church should all be ours; ours should be her victories, her sufferings, her pains.

This is not mere poetry, but a theological, spiritual and juridical reality. We have given ourselves to the Church, and the Church has made us hers; our vows are three golden cords binding our life to the Church, by which the Church has made our life her own and we have made the Church's life ours. *Thus, I have no interests other than those of the Church.*

Our prayer must be the prayer of the Church, and the prayer of the Church must be ours; the apostolate of the Church must be our apostolate, and our apostolate must be the apostolate of the Church. There is a fusion of personalities in the here and now.

MANIFESTATION OF THE CHURCH

Our institute must be an ecclesial institute, whose manner of thinking and judging is the Church's manner of thinking and judging; our mentality must be the very mentality of the Church.

Not long ago, the Holy Father deplored the fact that in certain quarters ideas and judgments vastly different from those of the Church have been circulating.

We cannot sever our personality from that of the Church, nor our mentality from hers; therefore, the need is always more strongly felt that during the juniorate the thought, life and necessities of the Church be studied even in the social sphere, along with moral and social problems, in order to evaluate all in the light of the Church.

God and with our brethren is Jesus Christ, who perpetuates Himself in the Church. This is true, but at the side of Jesus we find Mary.

We must be grateful to the Lord for inspiring Pope Paul VI to proclaim Mary most holy the Mother of the Church: mother of shepherds, mother of the faithful, mother of religious, mother of priests—mother universal.

A current of joy ran through the entire conciliar assembly at the proclamation of Mary as Mother of the Church. This act was completely the initiative of Paul VI. Taking the proclamation of Mary as Mother of the Church and our mother upon himself as his own personal responsibility as Christ's Vicar—the Holy Father rendered us this service, and Our Lady this homage.

Mary is the mother of us religious by a special title, for we are bound to her in a particular manner, through Jesus and through the Church.

We must endeavor to live this reality, and to derive great profit from it; we must endeavor to become reflections of her, and to let ourselves be drawn by her: "Draw me to you, O my Mother, so that I may walk in the pathway of your virtues."

Let us ask her to enable us to share in her ecclesial life, with regard to God and our neighbor.

MOTHER OF RELIGIOUS

It may be clearly and vividly seen in Mary's life that hers is a life in and for the Church, in dependence upon the Church—as it may also be seen that she lives the Church in herself. She is our model and guide.

The Blessed Virgin holds a position in the Church. The constitution *Lumen Gentium* ends with chapter 8, on Mary, who is the summit and crowning glory of the entire Church. Mary has a special place in the Church: on the one hand she is its mother; on the other, she is its most choice portion, its most exquisite, perfect and mature fruit.

Mary's position in the Church is centered in Jesus. In Jesus and with Him the Blessed Virgin is related to the three Divine Persons, because of that bond which she has, with and through Jesus, with the Church.

He was to be the Savior, the Redeemer and Head of the Church, the angel declared when he announced the incarnation to Mary. And Mary, Mother of Jesus, is our mother. In Jesus she encounters us, and in Him we encounter her.

All relations with the Divine Persons pass through Jesus, and thus all our relations with God and with our neighbor must pass through Him.

The stronger our bond with Jesus, the stronger our bond with our brethren.

Mary presides over all the life of the Church. She it is who must generate us; she it is who must form and mold us in the Church. We are carried in the bosom of the Church and in the bosom of Mary. Everyone greatly needs the Blessed Mother. Every Christian life must pass through Mary, not by absolute necessity, but because God has so willed it. Mary is necessary as a mother is necessary to a child, but she must have a special place if the degree of similarity to Jesus is to be more complete and perfect.

If the religious life is configuration with Christ in a more full and perfect manner, who will actualize in us this similarity to Jesus in His passion, in His sacrifice, in the sensitivity of His charity? What artist will paint this resemblance in strokes of gold? Only Mary—she who is the mother and co-redemptrix, completely associated with Jesus.

MODEL OF ECCLESIAL LIFE

Mary is an historical reality who is ever living and perpetuates herself and works continually. She must have a place in our life, and we can never exaggerate our devotion to her and our imitation of her.

A text of St. Ambrose is to be found in *Perfectae Caritatis* (this being the one citation found in the decree). It is an invitation to fidelity, to a renewal to be actualized through the intercession of "the Virgin Mary, the gentle Mother of God, *'whose life is a model for all.'*" In interceding, the Blessed Virgin not only prays for us, but also presents herself to the Lord and presents herself to us as a mirror for all, as an exemplar for all.

Thus does *Lumen Gentium*, n. 46, affirm that the Blessed Mother was the first to reproduce the image of

Jesus in the Church. The form of life which we wish to reproduce is the form that Mary was the first to live.

Mary presents herself as an epitome of spiritual life so eloquent, obliging and attractive, that in following her it is not difficult to outline a program of formation.

Mary lived for the Church. Who has given more to the Church than Mary? And who, after Jesus, has immolated herself more completely for the Church than Mary? Her entire life was for Jesus and for the Church. She gave not only her life, but also her divine Son.

The Blessed Virgin is mother of Jesus the Redeemer. Not blindly, but knowingly, she was associated with the divine plan. By means of the angel the Lord was clear and explicit: "You will conceive and bring forth a son; and you shall call his name Jesus. He shall be great...and he shall be king over the house of Jacob forever; and of his kingdom there shall be no end..." (Lk. 1:31-33).

Knowingly, Mary said her "yes," and gave herself through her consecration of poverty, of virginity and of obedience.

The women of Israel put much store on maternity, and Mary consecrated her virginity to God. Through this gift of self to the Lord, she was in a position to offer Him something more precious than what an earthly mother could give.

HANDMAID OF THE WHOLE CHRIST

The earthly life of the Blessed Virgin was consumed for the Church. In every circumstance of her life she is in the act of offering with Jesus: in the temple, in the flight into Egypt, and on and on, all the way to Calvary. She is there to offer herself and to offer Jesus.

Our offering too, is united to that of Mary, who gave and continues to give everything she had and has. Mary lived for Jesus and for the Church; that is, for the whole Christ.

Because of this we should have great confidence and trust in Mary—a trust which, as Pope Paul VI says, we must base on doctrinal foundations.

The greatness of Mary appears when we consider her in the immense mystery of the Church—above all, in that moment in which she is called to be the mother of the Head and of the members and is admitted into the most intimate, profound and close communion with all the redemptive action of Jesus. She responds with obedience: "Behold the handmaid of the Lord, may it be done unto me according to your word."

Obedience is a "yes," an act of love. The more one loves, the more one places himself at the disposition of the loved one. In fact, love leads to a union of wills, to a union of life.

To belong to the Church, to immolate oneself for the Church, is to become a servant of love of the Church. *To serve is to reign.*

And truly, what rights could we boast of in regard to God? There is only one: the right to His love, which obliges us to a complete donation; it commits us totally.

PERFECT IMAGE OF THE CHURCH

Let us renew our consecration to Mary, and she will bind us ever more closely to the Church. She teaches us to live with the Church, in communion with the Church's holiness, and she teaches us to realize the vocation of the Church to sanctity, for, as we are reminded in *Lumen Gentium,* n. 65:

"In the most holy Virgin the Church has already reached that perfection whereby she is without spot or wrinkle."

The Church has attained perfection in Mary, and Mary has made her own the perfection of the Church. She "shines forth to the whole community of the elect as the model of virtue."

Mary is the mother of Jesus, but she is also the first of the redeemed. The mystery of Mary is varied. She is mother. She is daughter.

Mary made the life of the Church her own, and the Church made the holiness of Mary hers.

Mary made the saving plan of God her own and made the vocation of the Church her own in all its dimensions — that of prayer, of prophecy and of apostolate. The ecclesial life of the Blessed Mother is a precious pearl in which new riches are always to be discovered.

Mary assimilated the Church's vocation into her thoughts, into her will, into her tastes; she studied the words of Jesus, making them hers, conserving them, meditating on them in her heart; she gathered up the actions and deeds of Jesus; she is the mirror for the Church, which she reflects in her dual role as mother and daughter.

Her every deed, her every gesture, is a deed and gesture of the Church; her every thought reflects the thought of the Church.

She points out to us how our thought must meet the thought of the Church, how our will should harmonize itself with that of the Church, and how our every action sould reflect the actions of the Church.

CONSECRATION TO MARY IS CONSECRATION
TO THE CHURCH

"Cost what it may, I stand with the Church": this total fidelity should be our constant attitude. With the consecration to Mary let us begin anew to live our ecclesial life, with Mary, through Mary and in Mary. Thus we will live with the Church, through the Church and in the Church.

The infallible means for living a perfect ecclesial life according to the directives of the Council is precisely a filial devotion to Mary. If the Blessed Virgin is mother, we must be children; if her maternity is ceaselessly in action, our filial piety toward her should be enduring and should express itself in dependence, attachment, availability and docility.

Let us give ourselves, mind, heart and will, to Mary. She is the mold of God (St. Augustine) and of the Church.

Was not the Church born of her? Yes. Then, we place ourselves in her and remain in her. The more Marian we are, the more shall we be ecclesial; the more we wish to be ecclesial, the more we must be Marian.

Let us thank God and remain faithful to our Marian consecration at any cost, with every effort. The Marian character is the Christological and ecclesial character.

May all religious feel themselves united to Mary. May their consecration to her draw all their institutes together and link them with ever stronger Marian and ecclesial ties.

DAUGHTERS OF ST. PAUL

In Massachusetts
    50 St. Paul's Avenue
        Boston, Mass. 02130
    172 Tremont Street
        Boston, Mass. 02111
    381 Dorchester Street
        So. Boston, Mass. 02127
    325 Main Street
        Fitchburg, Mass. 01420

In New York
    78 Fort Place
        Staten Island, N.Y. 10301
    625 East 187th Street
        Bronx, N.Y. 10458
    525 Main Street
        Buffalo, N.Y. 14203

In Connecticut
    202 Fairfield Avenue
        Bridgeport, Conn. 06603

In Ohio
    141 West Rayen Avenue
        Youngstown, Ohio 44503
    415 Euclid Avenue
        Cleveland, Ohio 44114

In Florida
    2700 Biscayne Blvd.
        Miami, Florida 33137

In Louisiana
    2814 South Carrollton Avenue
        New Orleans, La. 70118
    86 Bolton Avenue
        Alexandria, La. 71301

In Texas
    114 East Main Plaza
        San Antonio, Texas 78205

In California
    1570 Fifth Avenue
        San Diego, Calif. 92101
    278 - 17th Street
        Oakland, Calif. 94612

In Canada
    8885 Blvd. Lacordaire
    St. Leonard Deport-Maurice
        Montreal, Canada
    1003 St. Clair Avenue West
        Toronto, Canada

In Australia
    58 Abbotsford Road
        Homebush N.S.W., Australia

In Africa
    Box 4392
        Kampala, Uganda

In England
    20 Beauchamp Place
        London, S.W. 3, England

In India
    Water Field Road Extension
    Plot N. 143
        Bandra, India

In Philippine Islands
    No. 326 Lipa City
        Philippine Islands